Dazed, Nate kept moving d

Despite the blood dripping fro
the grisly hole in his arm.

Oil spilled across the wooden floor and ignited.

Grabbing the knife, Nate rushed to Sara and cut her bindings. "Are you all right?"

Sara nodded. "Just need to get the blood flowing again." She shook her arms out and cautiously tried to stand. Nate scooped her up into his arms.

The house was a tinderbox of dry and rotted lumber, and the blaze had already climbed the walls to the ceiling. Choking on smoke, unable to see anything, he made his way back to the front door.

When he was almost there, an earsplitting crack sounded, and Nate looked up just as the second floor crashed down on top of him.

RESOLUTE BODYGUARD

LESLIE MARSHMAN

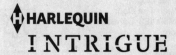

To Red

For all the times you've been an unofficial
background brainstormer.

Recycling programs
for this product may
not exist in your area.

ISBN-13: 978-1-335-59167-8

Resolute Bodyguard

Copyright © 2024 by Leslie Marshman

For questions and comments about the quality of this book, please contact us
at CustomerService@Harlequin.com.

TM and ® are trademarks of Harlequin Enterprises ULC.

Harlequin Enterprises ULC
22 Adelaide St. West, 41st Floor
Toronto, Ontario M5H 4E3, Canada
www.Harlequin.com

Printed in Lithuania

MIX
Paper | Supporting
responsible forestry
FSC® C021394

Multi-award-winning author **Leslie Marshman** writes novels featuring strong heroines, the heroes who love them and the bad guys who fear them. She called Denver home until she married a Texan without reading the fine print. Now she lives halfway between Houston and Galveston and embraces the humidity. When Leslie's not writing, you might find her camping at a lake, fishing pole in one hand and a book in the other. Visit her at www.lesliemarshman.com, www.Facebook.com/lesliemarshmanauthor, www.Instagram.com/leslie_marshman or @lesliemarshman on Twitter.

Books by Leslie Marshman

Harlequin Intrigue

The Protectors of Boone County, Texas

Resolute Justice
Resolute Aim
Resolute Investigation
Resolute Bodyguard

Scent Detection

Visit the Author Profile page at Harlequin.com.

CAST OF CHARACTERS

Nate Reed—The only Reed to not join the Boone County Sherrif's Department, Nate left town right after high school. After learning the personal security business from the ground up, he and a partner opened their own company in California, catering to Hollywood's elite. He came home last year for his father's funeral and stayed for family business.

Sara Bennett—The Travis County assistant district attorney loves her life in Austin, Texas. But when her boss pulls her biggest case out from under her and her best friend calls from Resolute begging her to take over as county judge, she jumps at the opportunity for another big step toward her career goal.

Cassie Reed—The oldest Reed sibling as well as the Boone County sheriff since her father's death. Cassie's a stickler for the rules, but when their judge drops dead, she's willing to take a little detour around the letter of the law to fill the vacancy.

Adam Reed—Chief deputy to his sister, the sheriff, Adam takes his job seriously.

Noah Reed—A Boone County deputy, Noah's the comic relief in the family. And he knows things about his twin, Nate, that no one else does.

Chapter One

"We call Nathaniel Reed, Your Honor."

Nate strode to the stand and swore to tell the truth before sitting on the hard wooden seat. It was a late Friday afternoon, and he gazed at the sea of faces filling the small courtroom. The divorce trial of Skip and Mitzi Stoddard, the reigning high muckety-mucks of Boone County, was the biggest attraction to hit Resolute, Texas, in years.

The day had been long, the room growing ever warmer as the two lawyers tried to corral their clients and avoid contempt charges.

"Mr. Reed, did you witness an altercation between my client and her husband on September twelfth of this year?" Mitzi's attorney asked.

"I did." But he hadn't planned to testify on Mitzi's behalf when he tried to break up a physical fight between the couple in the Chute's parking lot.

"Please tell us what happened that night." The out-of-town attorney who specialized in newsworthy divorces gave Nate a smarmy grin.

He thinks he has this in the bag.

"As I walked toward the restaurant, I heard arguing and saw Mr. and Mrs. Stoddard beneath one of the parking lot lights. He pushed her, she slapped him and then he punched her in the face."

Gasps swept across the room like the wave at a sports stadium.

"What happened next?" the attorney asked.

"I rushed over to see if Mrs. Stoddard needed help, but before I reached her, she'd landed a punch of her own. I separated them, but they both told me to mind my own business."

"To clarify, Mr. Stoddard laid hands on his wife first. Correct?"

Having worked as a bodyguard before opening his own security-and-protection company back in California, Nate had been trained on how to testify at trials. "Their altercation began before I saw them, so I have no way of knowing who started it."

Mitzi's attorney angled a glare at Nate.

Skip's deep baritone broke the silence as he jumped to his feet. "See? I told you she started it."

"Counsel, control your client." Judge Harmon always gave one warning. But never more than one.

Skip's lawyer, famous throughout Texas for winning felony cases, pulled on his client's sleeve in an attempt to yank him back into his seat.

"I didn't start it. He did!" Mitzi stood and pointed at Skip. "And he threatened to kill me."

Her attorney rushed back to their table. "Sit down *now*."

Judge Harmon banged his gavel.

"The hell you say." Skip turned to face her.

Mitzi took a step toward Skip, and her lawyer wrapped his arms around her waist from behind to hold her back. She pulled at her attorney's hands, her long nails digging bloody trails across them.

Judge Harmon banged his gavel. "Order! Order in the court!"

Mitzi broke free and charged Skip, who slid around the far side of his table. Mitzi followed him, and both lawyers ran to separate their clients. The bailiff, a middle-aged woman who was as much a courtroom fixture as the judge, rushed to intervene.

Mitzi slapped Skip.

Judge Harmon stood, an angry frown on his reddening face. Nate hoped the judge's blood pressure medication was working.

Skip threw a punch meant for Mitzi. She ducked, and her attorney took it on the chin.

Judge Harmon banged his gavel again and again. "Bailiff, take them both into custody. Seeing as it's Friday, they'll be spending the weekend in jail. We'll attempt this again next week."

Mitzi straightened and slugged Skip with an uppercut that sent him sprawling backward into his lawyer.

Cassie Reed, Nate's sister and the Boone County sheriff, raced from the public viewing area to assist the bailiff. Nate glanced at the judge, now an alarming shade of maroon, before he swung over the edge of the witness box and ran to help. The bailiff fought to get Skip off his attorney, while Cassie moved behind Mitzi to cuff her. But the woman was too quick, lunging for the bailiff's sidearm and pulling it from its holster.

"Gun!" Cassie yelled.

Mitzi swung the barrel toward Skip and pulled the trigger a second after he dove back to the floor. Nate tackled the woman, grabbing the gun from her hand as they landed in a tangle of limbs. At the same time, a piercing shriek filled the room. Everyone froze, and Nate looked toward its source. The shot had grazed the court reporter's arm. But instead of looking at her own wound, the stenographer's look of horror was turned toward the judge.

Judge Harmon lay collapsed across his bench, one arm outstretched, his gavel teetering on the edge.

Cassie tossed Nate zip cuffs for Mitzi, then helped the bailiff flip Skip onto his stomach and cuff him before calling for an ambulance and deputies. "Nate, I need you." She headed toward the judge.

Putting nothing past the woman he'd just cuffed, Nate sat her in a chair and used another pair of ties to secure her to the attorney's table. Then he followed his sister behind the judge's bench, where she checked for a pulse.

"He's already gone." Cassie held the chair while Nate maneuvered the portly judge, a fan of weekly church pancake-and-bacon breakfasts, back into it without letting him slide to the floor.

They examined him for holes and blood, then agreed he hadn't been hit by the bullet ricocheting.

"Heart attack?" Nate asked. "He was passing maroon and approaching burgundy when I joined the melee."

"Maybe. Might have been an aneurysm or a stroke. We'll let the medical examiner tell us."

Another commotion in the courtroom caught Nate's attention. His brothers, Chief Deputy Adam Reed and Deputy Noah Reed, strode down the center aisle and took possession of the Stoddards.

Nate surveyed the room. All four Reed siblings, two cuffed spouses, one frazzled bailiff, a winged court reporter and a dead magistrate.

He looked at Cassie. "We're gonna need another judge."

SARA BENNETT STAGGERED into her penthouse apartment and dropped her briefcase and purse on the entryway floor.

Kicking off her heels, she detoured through the kitchen for a glass of wine on the way to her fashionable, yet comfortable, living room.

After another ten-hour day as a Travis County prosecuting attorney, she looked forward to the weekend. Not that she wouldn't still be working, but trial prep at home in athleisure and fuzzy socks beat a day at the office in a suit and heels every time.

She'd just settled onto her couch when a text notification chimed on her cell phone. Sara fished it out of her blazer pocket, glanced at the screen and cursed, her hand tightening around her wine glass.

enjoy ur weekend while u can

She had no idea who was texting her, taunting her. Before joining the district attorney's office, she'd been told things like this—angry phone calls and emails—could happen. What bothered her was that she'd been receiving the texts for several weeks, and they were coming in on her personal cell.

Most likely, they had nothing to do with her job. Probably a wrong number who never figured out their mistake. That was what she'd convinced herself of anyway.

Sara gazed through her living room's wall of windows. Austin's lights glowed in a view stretching out before her, Friday's nightlife just starting to spring into action. And she didn't mind one bit enjoying it from the comfort of her home. Put her in court, questioning a witness in a criminal felony case, and she didn't miss a beat. But stick her on a bar stool in a club trying to make small talk with a stranger, and she disappeared like a redacted sentence in a legal brief.

When her cell rang with "I Shot the Sheriff," she answered it on speaker. "Cassie. What's happening out in the boondocks these days?"

"Oh, you know, the usual. Drunk-and-disorderlies at the local dive bar, speeding tickets in school zones, the plaintiff in a divorce trial shooting off a gun in the courtroom and the judge dropping dead from a heart attack."

"Good one." Sara wandered into her bedroom, tossed her phone on the bed and slipped out of her skirt and jacket. When Cassie stayed silent, she asked, "You're joking, right?"

"I wish. Happened last Friday—craziest trial I ever witnessed."

After dropping her blouse in the laundry basket, Sara pulled on a pair of leggings and an oversized fleece top. Grabbing her phone, she padded back out to the couch. "Who was the plaintiff trying to shoot?"

"Her husband. Thankfully, she missed him but winged the court reporter. It was sometime during the brouhaha when the judge collapsed."

"I may be prosecuting violent offenders in a big city criminal court, but li'l old Resolute always sounds way more exciting." Sara sipped her wine. "Did I tell you I've been assigned my first murder trial?"

"You sound enthusiastic." Cassie's tone sounded the opposite, which disappointed Sara. Usually her friend was her biggest cheerleader.

"I am. It feels good to finally be respected by my boss. For so long, he handed me cases he considered less important. But my conviction rate's impressive, if I do say so myself." She was proud of that rate—not because of the high number, but because the people she put away deserved to be off the streets.

"You always *were* focused on your goals. Your grandfather must be so proud of you."

Sara smiled at that.

"So… I guess I should tell you why I've called." Cassie cleared her throat. "I was hoping I might entice you to take a break from lawyering and come be our replacement judge."

Sara hadn't known what to expect, but it definitely wasn't this. "I've already got a job I love, Cass. And I wouldn't even qualify. I haven't lived in Boone County for the last six months."

"We might have a way around that. Since you officially became involved with the Boone County Youth Program eight months ago, Bree's been receiving mail addressed to you at her place. You'd just need to change your driver's license and voter registration immediately."

"Cassandra Reed!" Sara's voice rang out in her high-ceilinged penthouse. "Are you telling me that you, the most by-the-book stickler I've ever known, are saying you're willing to go *around* something? Bishop must be rubbing off on you."

"I need to run it past the county commissioners, but I'm sure we can make it work. I just wanted to ask you first." Cassie's voice dropped into a whisper. "And off the record, my husband's ability to skirt the rules as a PI might have influenced me a little."

Sara wandered out to her balcony and gazed at the carpet of lights beneath her. She wanted to do her friend a favor, but not at the cost of her own career.

And then there was Nate. Cassie had told her a while back that he'd spent a good portion of the last year or so in Texas, but she hadn't mentioned if he was back in California now. Sara hadn't seen or talked to him since their brief fling a decade ago and wasn't sure how she felt about seeing him now—if he *was* still in Resolute.

She did think about him, though, and probably more often

than she should. She'd discovered those first-love feelings and memories never quite disappeared completely, and every time Nate crossed her mind they still tugged at her heart.

"I'm honored that you thought of me, but there's gotta be someone down there who wants the job. What about whoever lost the last election?"

"Judge Harmon has run unopposed every four years for the last thirty-two. No one down here wants to be— Oops. Guess I shouldn't have said that last part. Seriously, you'd love it. There's even a house that comes with the job, so you won't have to rent a place. And it would only be until the next election takes place in a few months."

It wasn't the judicial position Sara was working toward, but it *was* a judgeship. Was accepting the offer enough to give up her career with the DA's office?

Was it enough to risk facing her unresolved emotions about Nate? She'd never told her friend about sleeping with him during that spring-break visit. Maybe because he was Cassie's little brother and Sara had worried it would damage their friendship. Or maybe because she'd always felt a little guilty about how she'd ended things with him.

Sara swallowed the last of her wine. "I'm sorry, but I have to say no. My life is perfect right now. I love living in the city. Plus, I've got a big trial coming up, and there's no way I can back out of it. It'll be the biggest one so far in my career."

"Well, I tried."

"I do appreciate you thinking of me. It's just not a great time to break my momentum at work."

"No worries. I'm glad everything's going so well for you. You're still invited for Thanksgiving if you want to come down and overdose on family."

"Thanks. Sounds like you'll have quite a crowd this year, what with all the pairing-up y'all have been doing lately."

Cassie chuckled. "Yep, the Reed family is growing. But we always have room for you."

Sara gave up on her friend volunteering information about Nate and bit the bullet. "Is Nate still in town for the holidays, or did he have to go back to the coast and miss the feast?" *Hopefully that sounded casual rather than interested.*

"I think he has a quick round trip planned, but he'll be here for Thanksgiving. Unfortunately he'll be heading back to California permanently in December, so he won't be home for Christmas." Cassie sighed. "It's been nice having him around. I'm going to miss him."

"What a shame." *I'll have to face him if I go for Thanksgiving.* "Turkey Day's not for another three weeks, right? Let me check my trial schedule, and I'll let you know if I can make it." Sara's phone beeped with an incoming call. "I have to take this. Talk soon."

She ended one call and accepted the new one. "Hello?"

"Hi, Sara. It's Alton."

She went back inside and closed the sliding glass door to cut off the background traffic noise. Calls from the district attorney were always important, especially on a Friday night. "Alton. What can I do for you?"

"It's about the Singleton trial coming up."

Relieved that she could speak confidently about her preparation, Sara smiled. "I've finished all the—"

"I'm sorry, but you won't be first chair. I'm prosecuting the case."

"I'm almost finished with the trial prep. I planned on working all weekend so next week could be devoted to jury-selection details."

"I appreciate all your hard work, Sara. But I've been instructed to take over."

Sara controlled her anger. "Will I be second chair?"

"I can't have an ADA who accepts plea deals anywhere near the case. It's a delicate situation."

"I've rarely made plea deals, and I definitely had no intention of making one in this case. Singleton belongs in prison." She paced as she spoke. "Look, Alton, I'm ready for this trial. And you know how much it means to me."

"I know. And I *am* sorry. But I just got off the phone with the governor, and he wants an experienced prosecutor who will send the defense attorney home in tears every night. Apparently a senator has been in his ear about this trial." He sighed. "It's all politics, Sara. Nothing against your work or you personally. I promise I'll assign you the next murder trial we get."

She could almost hear the unspoken part of that sentence: *that doesn't involve politicians.*

"Messenger everything you have at home on the case to my home tonight. I need to jump on this immediately."

"I'll do it as soon as we hang up." Sara ended the call before she damaged their working relationship with words she'd regret.

She strode into the kitchen, grabbed the bottle of wine and returned to the couch. Damn him. She refilled her glass and took a long drink of the cold Riesling. She wouldn't cry. She never cried. But she sure as hell wanted to punch something. She'd been working on the Singleton case for months, along with other smaller cases. And now she was supposed to just hand over her piles of investigation and preparation to her boss, who would waltz into the courtroom with a slam-dunk case?

She didn't want to do it, but she would. She had to. Because the scumbag defendant needed to be locked up. Because she wasn't about to get blamed for Alton losing the case due to lack of preparation on Sara's part. And because she just wasn't wired that way.

As she walked across the room she called up her favorite Etta James album on her cell and connected to her living room soundbar. Returning to the couch, she picked up the remote for her gas fireplace and turned it on. Listening to the soulful blues, staring into the real flames dancing among the fake logs, Sara considered her options. She wasn't one to make spur-of-the-moment decisions. Her entire life had been planned with care since the day she turned fourteen.

If she swallowed her pride and went back to her heavy workload of small cases, she had Alton's promise of a future murder case. Plus, she enjoyed working with him. She'd made it a practice to never burn bridges behind her, and she dreaded setting fire to the one she had with Alton.

On the other hand, if she took the position in Boone County now, when she returned to Austin with a judgeship added to her résumé her opportunities would be wide open. She could be one big step closer to her dream of being a district judge, like her grandfather had been. Except in Travis County, home of the state capitol.

She grabbed her cell and pulled up her favorites list.

Cassie answered with, "Please don't tell me you can't make Thanksgiving."

"Oh, I'll be there." She would just have to deal with Nate if he was home for the holiday. And if he was still basically living there, well—like Pops always said—never trouble trouble until trouble troubles you. She took one more sip of liquid courage. "And about that judge vacancy..."

NATE STROLLED INTO the kitchen of the Reed ranch, and all talk ceased. No family dinner had been scheduled, yet Cassie was leaning against the counter, discussing something with Adam and Noah.

"We were talking about how hard it is to find someone to take Judge Harmon's place," Cassie said.

"Have you talked to the county commissioners yet?" Nate picked up the open can of nuts on the counter and shook some into his hand. "Surely someone must want the position and was just waiting so they wouldn't have to run against Harmon."

"I *have* talked to them. But so far no volunteers have stepped forward." Cassie popped a cashew into her mouth. "But it's only been a week since Harmon died. We'll find a replacement."

Nate shrugged. "If they want me to testify for the divorce trial again, it better happen soon. I'm still heading back to California in a few weeks, and I'll be out there indefinitely this time."

"I'm not sure Mitzi's lawyer will call you again as a witness. He wasn't happy with your magnificently vague answer last time, and I'm not sure it matters now that she's charged with attempted murder and aggravated assault." Cassie crunched another nut. "If she doesn't accept a plea deal, her trial for the new charges will be handled by the district court, and we'll all be called as witnesses. But that won't be happening any time soon."

Adam tasted the chili he was stirring, adding in more spices, and changed the topic. "So you think this big contract coming up will put Reed & Franklin Security on the map?"

"We're already on the map, bro." The only thing Nate got defensive about was his company. He and his partner,

Matt Franklin, had busted their butts to bring in elite clients who needed bodyguards, security and protection. And word of mouth had done its magic in record time. "But this contract is with a big company with an even bigger budget. We'd be able to hire more security professionals and expand the business."

"I'm proud of you." Cassie's eyes filled with big-sister love. "Dad would be, too."

Nate bit his tongue, not wanting to ruin the evening. He and their father had butted heads often, which was why he'd left town shortly after high school. It was enough that his sister and brothers believed in him. "Did I miss the memo about a late family dinner tonight?"

"It's just siblings. And since when is seven thirty late for any kind of Reed dinner?" Adam put a pan of cornbread into the oven. "At least I don't have to make a special veggie chili for Bishop." He raised a brow toward Cassie.

"Hey, not my fault my husband's a health freak. Speaking of health, isn't it about time to toast ours?"

"Past time, if you ask me." Noah retrieved four longneck bottles of beer from the fridge, pried off the caps and passed them around.

They tipped their bottles toward each other and drank.

Nate finally registered the otherwise quiet house. "Where are Rachel and the kids?"

Adam straightened from checking the cornbread. "She and Bree had some youth program business tonight, and they decided to go out for dinner afterward. And Martina wanted some time with her grandkids."

"Like she doesn't get some every day babysitting." Cassie laughed. "You really lucked out in the future-mother-in-law lottery with her."

"Tell me about it. She loves taking care of Daisy, but

there's not much conversation happening with a one-year-old. Now that Brad's in kindergarten, I think she misses spending all day with him." Adam looked at his siblings, all three standing around doing nothing. "Y'all better get cracking on the toppings because this chili is just about ready."

A flurry of cheese grating, jalapeño slicing and table setting commenced. By the time the cornbread and pot of chili were set on the table, everyone was seated except Adam. He ladled his famous Texas all-beef-no-beans chili into bowls and passed them around.

Cassie's phone rang while she was still blowing on her first steaming spoonful. "Be right back." She disappeared into the kitchen.

A few minutes later the brothers heard a whoop, then Cassie returned with a triumphant smile on her face.

"We not only have an additional guest for Thanksgiving, but we've got ourselves a judge."

"That was Sara?" Adam asked.

"Yep." Cassie scooped that first bite of chili into her mouth, following it with a nibble of cornbread.

Noah let out a loud laugh and looked at Nate. "Bro…"

There was only one Sara who Cassie would invite to Thanksgiving. The Sara who was a lawyer in Austin. The same Sara who'd stolen his heart before breaking it more than ten years ago. "Are you talking about Sara Bennett?"

Cassie nodded. "You remember her, right? I brought her home for spring break one year." She took a sip of beer.

Oh, he remembered her all right.

Sara's rejection had happened when he was admittedly immature, when the rest of his life had been in turmoil. He'd felt like a fool, and whether or not she even remembered, he couldn't forget.

Cassie frowned. "It's too bad you'll be leaving for good so

soon after she gets here." Then the frown turned into a smile. "But at least you'll have Thanksgiving together."

"Ah, just like Paris." Noah was the only Reed who knew about Nate and Sara's brief romance during her long-ago visit. "You've always had spring break, but now you'll always have Thanksgiving."

Nate avoided his brother's eyes. This was one of the times having a twin in tune with his thoughts sucked.

"When's she arriving?" Adam asked.

"Monday." Cassie reached for her beer. "I hope it's okay—I told her she can stay here until the judge's mansion is ready for her to move into." When Boone County was established in the late 1800s, the first county judge had built an enormous, stately home within walking distance of the courthouse. With no relatives, and serving until his death, he'd deeded the house to the county on the condition it be offered as a home to every subsequent Boone County judge. "We'll need to sort out and pack up Harmon's personal effects and have the place cleaned."

Adam nodded. "We've got the room."

"Perfect." Cassie grinned.

"Yeah. Just perfect." Nate rolled his eyes mentally when no one but Noah caught his sarcastic tone.

His sister looked at him. "It'll give you two a chance to get reacquainted. I think you're the only one who didn't see her when she was here for the youth center ribbon cutting this summer." Cassie pushed back her chair and scooped a second serving of chili into her bowl. "I'm looking forward to catching up with her myself. I guess she's got some juicy stories she can't wait to tell me."

Chapter Two

"Hi, Sara."

The handsome man who opened the Reeds' front door smiled, and Sara forgot to take her next breath. Nate's angled cheekbones and strong jaw had replaced the softer features of his younger self, but she'd recognize him anywhere. Especially since she'd cyberstalked him a little.

Her lips automatically curled into a return smile as she finally sucked in air. "Nate. It's been a long time."

Nate opened the door all the way. "Come on in. I'll grab your luggage for you." He took a step toward the porch as she crossed the threshold.

Turning to face each other so there was room to pass, Sara inhaled his scent. No longer a teenage boy wearing his father's Old Spice to impress a girl, Nate smelled of fresh air and sun-dried laundry.

"There's no need to get it right now." She lifted her gaze, meeting his dark brown eyes. "I may stay at a hotel instead." She moved past him into the living room.

"Unless you want a long commute, the closest you'll come to a hotel are a few rundown motels between Resolute and Victoria. We do have Doc's Motor Court here in town, but I think you'll be more comfortable staying at the house."

"Hmm." Sara gazed at the well-worn leather furniture

and wooden beams overhead. More rustic than she was used to, but charming. She'd loved this house the last time she'd stayed here, mainly because of the feeling of family she'd experienced for the first time in her life.

Her own parents had been self-absorbed while playing at being jet-setters, leaving it to the nanny and housekeeper and cook to raise their daughter. But the Reeds were like the families she'd read about in books as a child. The type of family she'd always longed for, even before she'd met them.

"Then I accept the invitation to stay here, as long as I'm not intruding." Sara sat on the couch, unable to relax until Nate sat across from her in a leather recliner. But then she couldn't pull her eyes away from him. He'd had a great physique even when she had first met him. The Henley he wore now revealed even larger biceps than she remembered. His chest, a broad expanse of muscles, stretched the shirt wide before it narrowed and clung to what Sara would bet her favorite pair of Louboutin heels were granite-hard six-pack abs.

"Big change, moving down here," Nate said. "Was it hard giving up the DA position in Austin?"

She hid the momentary spark of surprise that ricocheted through her brain. Though she'd thought of Nate often and Cassie had given her infrequent updates about the Reed brothers' lives, Sara had never imagined *him* knowing anything current about her life.

"It wasn't an easy decision. I enjoyed being a prosecutor. But I'm looking at this opportunity as a means to an end." She brushed at a piece of lint on the sleeve of her cashmere sweater. "And you? Your security company seems to be doing well."

His dark brown eyes widened, and she mentally kicked

herself. Cassie had only mentioned that he had his own business, and that was a few years ago. Sara had kept up with Nate's success by occasional online sleuthing.

He straightened in his chair. "It is. The last year's been difficult, with me spending so much time in Resolute. But between my partner in the office in California and me working remotely—as well as racking up frequent flier miles between here and there—we're still growing." The pride in his voice was clear.

"How did you decide on a career in security?" None of the articles about Nate or his company had mentioned its owner's path to success, other than the note in his bio about a background in security.

"I sort of fell into it." He crossed a boot onto the opposite knee, his thumb tapping a soundless rhythm on the chair arm as he seemed to run out of words.

Lord, save me from lulls in small talk. "How does someone fall into a career like that?"

"I headed west after I graduated, eventually got a job in Vegas as a bouncer. That led to a stint as a bodyguard with a security company. After learning everything there was to learn about the business, a buddy and I opened our own company in Southern California."

"You left Resolute when you were eighteen?" Sara willed her cheeks not to blush as the blunt question left her mouth. Being slightly older than Nate had seemed a big deal back then.

"I turned nineteen that June." His steady gaze bored into her. "A few months after we met."

So he *did* remember. Sara bit her tongue, refusing to be led into a discussion of their past. Best to just forget it. They were older now, wiser, traveling crosswise paths.

"Would you like some iced tea?" Nate's smooth baritone voice yanked her back to the present.

"I'd love some."

He disappeared into the kitchen as Sara sank back into the past.

Despite her instincts telling her she should, she didn't want to forget the past—that week, that night. It had been the first time anyone besides her grandfather had made her feel valued for just being herself. Not for being a good student or an overachiever. Not for being wealthy or having semi-famous parents.

But when spring break had drawn to a close, she'd panicked. She had seen the passionate look in Nate's eyes and known what was coming, just as she'd known she had no time for love. No desire for it. Not when she'd already sacrificed so much, worked so hard. Her life plan had already been set in stone, and she wouldn't allow it to be derailed. Especially by something as capricious as emotions. Still, she never wanted to forget what those emotions had felt like, however briefly they'd lasted.

Sara's phone dinged with a text notification, and a frustrated sigh escaped her as she pulled it from her purse. She'd had several during the drive from Austin, all from her boss. Make that *ex*-boss. And each one a question he could've answered for himself if he'd just read the case notes and research she'd sent him.

But when the screen lit up this time, it wasn't the district attorney.

u can run but u cant hide ill find you

A chill ran up Sara's spine, its icy tendrils reaching out, wrapping around her lungs, squeezing the breath from her.

The other texts she'd received from anonymous numbers had been annoying but harmless. She'd blocked them in the beginning, but each time they continued from new numbers.

This text seemed targeted at her, its message especially disturbing since she'd just left Austin.

Nate set a glass of tea on the table next to her, and still focused on the text, she startled.

"Everything okay?" Nate returned to his recliner.

"Sure." She tossed her phone back into her purse. "The DA I worked for keeps asking me questions about the case I was handling." For some reason, Sara didn't want to tell anyone about the texts. At least, not yet. She needed to think about it, poke it and probe it, try to figure out who was sending them. And why.

Nate's phone rang. "It's Cassie." He answered, and his side of the conversation consisted of a series of *uh-huh*s, *okay*s, and one *sure*. As he ended the call, he met Sara's eyes. "She's stuck on a case out in the boonies and won't make it home as early as she'd hoped. She asked me to take you over to the judge's mansion and see what you think about living there."

"Great." Relieved that she wouldn't be forced to make small talk all afternoon while the troubling text swirled in the back of her mind, Sara took a long drink from her tea, then stood. "Let's go."

As she buckled herself into Nate's passenger seat, she paused. "Wait, did you say *mansion*? Cassie just called it a house."

The corners of Nate's mouth kicked up in a wry grin. "It was considered a mansion in its day."

"How old *is* this place?"

"I wouldn't want to ruin the surprise for you." Nate

glanced at her, a sparkle in his eye. "But hey, it's free." He laughed as he turned from the Reed property onto the public road.

Good Lord. What have I gotten myself into?

Chapter Three

"This is it?" Sara stared out the passenger window at a huge house, set well back on an overgrown lot, about a half mile south of town. "You weren't kidding about its size."

Nate grinned. "It may not be the prettiest house around, but it is big. And that's probably the only drawback about this place—the maintenance. The judge in residence is responsible for the utilities and upkeep. Harmon obviously wasn't taking care of the grounds."

Assuming she'd inherited her parents' lack of nurturing skills, Sara had never owned so much as a single houseplant. "How big is the lot?"

"The house itself is on half an acre. The county owns the lots on either side, each one also half an acre. But they maintain those."

"Or maybe they don't." Sara's gaze drifted to the weeds and wildflowers as far as she could see. Maybe Judge Harmon had just decided to let his yard blend into the rest. She opened her door. "I'll look into local grounds-maintenance companies. Let's hope the interior looks better."

Since this was a temporary position, it made sense to stay here. But the mansion emitted a haunted-house aura, and Sara could imagine curtains of cobwebs and bats in the attic.

She started toward the long concrete walkway to the front porch.

"Wait." Nate grabbed her hand, his touch igniting a warm, tingling sensation. "Let me go first. I want to keep an eye out for rattlers and scorpions."

Eying the overgrowth on both sides of the path, she said, "Be my guest." Living on the top floor of one of Austin's tallest apartment buildings, most of the unsavory pests she'd run into were in the courtroom.

She followed Nate up onto the wraparound porch, and after he unlocked the front door, she walked into a dark foyer. The formal living room to their left was just as dim, and Sara strode across to the front windows and yanked open the heavy drapes. Dust motes danced in the bright sunlight, and she coughed from the stale smell.

After a quick look around at the dated furniture, Sara caught up with Nate, who had flipped up a light switch and wandered off to the right of the foyer. She found herself in an old-fashioned parlor, filled with uncomfortable-looking chairs and a matching love seat.

"Seriously, when was this place built?"

"I don't remember the exact year, but sometime in the late eighteen hundreds." Nate pointed at a small embroidered stool with silk fringe hanging from all four sides. "And it looks like some of this stuff came with the house."

"If not all of it." She dragged her finger through a quarter inch of dust on a hobnail glass lampshade. "Apparently the previous judge didn't spend much time in these downstairs rooms."

"His kids moved away when they became adults, and I imagine after his wife passed, he didn't need all this space." Nate surveyed the rest of the room. "Harmon was known to be a bit of a tightwad, so I doubt he had anyone come in to clean very often. Also probably why so many furnishings weren't updated."

Sara grimaced as she walked back to the foyer and took in the intricately carved staircase leading to the second floor. "I'm going upstairs."

Nate joined her before she reached the first landing. "Cassie was right about getting a professional cleaning crew in here."

"So he was a widower?" Sara paused at the top of the stairs and peered down the hallway in both directions.

"Yes. His wife died a long time ago. I remember my dad making us all go to the funeral." His tone softened. "First time I saw a dead body."

Her quick glance caught Nate's somber expression. Sara had no idea how many bodies he might have seen since but suspected he was thinking about his father, who'd been murdered the previous year. Wallace Reed had been the county sheriff for probably about as long as Harmon had ruled from the bench.

"I'm sorry I couldn't make it to your dad's service." She wanted to offer a hug but didn't. Best not to complicate their new, tenuous relationship with mixed signals. "Cassie mentioned that Wallace named you as the executor of his will."

"Go figure, right?" Nate twisted his mouth to the side. "I was the only one who didn't get along with him, and he chose me. I don't know…maybe he knew what a pain it was going to be."

"If he left a will, what's making it so difficult?"

"My mom. Dad never divorced her after she left. I doubt she would want anything from his estate since she obviously didn't even want us." He ran his fingers through his hair. "But the probate court ruled that we have to make

every possible effort to locate her and get a signed affida-
vit stating she has no claim."

"Do you know where she's been all this time?"

"I've got Bishop looking for her." He gave her a half-
hearted grin. "One of the good things about Cassie mar-
rying a PI."

"Do you know why your dad never divorced her?"

Nate's half smile disappeared completely. "She broke
his heart. I think at first he kept hoping she'd come back.
As time went on, he probably just didn't want to deal with
anything concerning her. So now I have to deal with it."
He ran his fingers through his hair again. "That's why I'm
flying back and forth so much. If not for handling the estate
and trying to help Adam, Noah and Cassie with their grief,
I'd have been back in California right after the funeral."

Heading toward the doors to her right, Sara suddenly
stopped and faced Nate. "Maybe that's why your dad chose
you as the executor."

His brows pulled together. "What are you talking about?"

"You said you stayed to help the others with their grief.
What about *yours*?"

"I grieved." Nate shrugged. "But I'd never been as close
to Dad as they were."

"Perhaps he knew you'd have to spend more time here,
which would give you all a chance to reconnect." She
arched a brow. "And maybe he knew you could deal with
his estate without being overcome by emotions."

He shook his head. "Wouldn't that mean he thought I
didn't love him?"

Sara tipped her head, searching his face. "*Did* you love
him?"

Nate scoffed. "Of course I did."

"Have you been able to take care of his will without

wallowing in grief?" When she didn't receive an answer, Sara added, "I think your father understood you better than you think. And trusting you with his will was his way of showing that. Showing that he loved you. That he knew you loved him."

While Nate stood as if his boots were nailed to the floor, Sara continued on to the first door and opened it, allowing him a moment to digest what she'd said. She entered a small bedroom, dust covers draped over the furniture. More doors opened onto similar rooms.

She turned and retraced her steps to where Nate still stood. "You going to help me check out the rest of the rooms, or what?" Without thinking, she grabbed his hand and tugged him toward the primary bedroom, trying to ignore the warmth of his fingers as they wrapped around hers.

NATE HAD FOLLOWED Sara's career online for years. But the posted pictures—professional headshots with perfect hair and full makeup—didn't hold a candle to the woman pulling him down the hall.

Her chin-length pale blond hair hung loose, framing her face—which, unless he was going blind, looked completely free of makeup. In jeans and a sweater, though a little upscale for Resolute, she looked ready for a hike in the woods. Exactly like the fresh-faced college student he'd never been able to forget.

Seeing Sara again proved less awkward than he'd imagined. So far, he had managed to avoid becoming tongue-tied in her presence. But he also hadn't planned on spending the whole day with her.

Fortunately, he'd be gone for the next two days, and after that she'd be living in the judge's mansion. Aside from Thanksgiving next week, they'd have little reason to run into each other before he returned to California for good. If he could just hold on to his cool a bit longer, they'd be out of each other's lives. Their paths were not aligned. Never had been, never would be. And he was fine with that.

As they entered the main bedroom, his nose twitched at the musty scent of the old house combined with dirty clothes piled on a chair.

"This room's going to need some changes." Sara opened one of the two wardrobes standing like sentinels on either side of the bathroom. "I guess if they're deep enough to hold Judge Harmon's suits, they'll work for my clothes. But it's going to be an adjustment from a walk-in closet."

"You could always buy some clothes racks and turn one of the smaller bedrooms into a closet." Hanging around Resolute with too much time on his hands, Nate had resorted to watching home-improvement and DIY shows.

Sara's eyes widened. "That's a great idea. Of course, I won't need as many dress suits here, especially with wearing a robe in court."

"Rumor had it that in the heat of summer, especially when the justice center's air-conditioning had a hard time keeping up, Harmon only wore a T-shirt and boxers under his robe."

She scrunched her nose. "Remind me to buy a new robe." She ambled into the bathroom. "Ooh, they updated in here."

Detecting a sarcastic tone, Nate poked his head into the en suite. "Impressive." A claw-foot soaking tub took up one corner of the large room, adapted to hold a shower head at one end. A plastic shower curtain hung behind the tub. His gaze rested on the sink countertop, littered only with the grooming items of an old man. It reeked of loneliness.

They returned to the first floor and headed to the back of the house, passing a large formal dining room to their right. The kitchen was on their left, the attached breakfast room behind it featuring a wall of windows looking out on a field of weeds and wildflowers.

Sara flashed a bright smile. "This room will be wonderful once the grounds are cleaned up. But I need to take a better look at that kitchen."

Sara eyed the appliances, her mouth set in a firm line. Though updated since the house had been built, they resembled those of the 1960s instead of the twenty-first century. "I wonder if the wattage can withstand a microwave and an espresso machine."

"We'll check before you plug anything in, but I'm sure they've kept the electrical panel current."

Sara laughed.

Nate raised his brows, puzzled.

"Electrical panel? Current?" She lifted one shoulder in a half shrug. "Hey, it was your pun."

Nate couldn't stop from rolling his eyes. "Unintentional, I assure you."

"Whatever happened to your sense of humor? You used to have a great one." At Sara's reference to the past, an uncomfortable silence descended. She developed a sudden interest in the avocado-green gas stove.

Silently agreeing the past should remain in the past, Nate crossed the kitchen and opened a door. Behind it was a utility room/pantry that sat next to the breakfast room. It held a washing machine, drier and a freezer, and the walls were lined with mostly bare shelves.

"Why is it so cold in here all of a sudden?" Sara leaned in through the doorway.

"Broken window. Be careful—there's glass all over the floor." Nate tipped his head toward the large opening on the outside wall. "I'll board it up before we leave, and we can get a replacement installed when I get back."

"How long do you suppose it's been like this?" Sara wrapped her arms around herself.

"I'm sure it happened since the judge died. Probably kids throwing a ball or something." He glanced around at shards of glass and muddy footprints. "There's no ball, and the window frame is free of glass, so they probably crawled in and retrieved it."

While Sara found a broom and swept up glass, Nate went to the detached garage, converted from the original carriage house, to hunt for a temporary window repair. He didn't want to worry Sara, but something felt off about his kids-with-a-ball theory. Between the high foundation of the house and the height of the window, not to mention no parks or other homes nearby, it was far more likely a vandal had broken out the window.

Nate blew out an exasperated breath. Regardless of who it had been, he'd suggest that Sara remain at the Reed ranch until he had time to check things out more thoroughly.

Coming up with nothing useful, he moved on to a large shed behind the garage that housed a riding mower and other landscaping tools. Finally finding a board large enough to cover the hole, Nate grabbed it, a hammer, nails and a collapsible ladder and rounded the outside of the house. As he propped the ladder against the wall, he noticed a mess of footprints in the ground below the window. More disturbing was the square impression amid them, as if someone had climbed up on something to see inside.

Nate climbed the ladder and began the mindless task of pounding nails, but his mind wouldn't quit working. Nothing of Judge Harmon's appeared to be missing, and other than the glass, no damage was apparent inside the home. So what had this mysterious Peeping Tom been up to?

After the board was in place, Nate returned everything else to the garage and looked around again. Nothing cube-shaped in there seemed strong enough to hold a person's weight. He checked the backyard, then went into the un-locked greenhouse. Besides dead plants in clay pots, stand-ing in rows like gravestones in a cemetery, he spotted an upside-down wooden crate. The boards didn't even flinch when he stepped up on it. Flipping it upright, the top edges were brown with dried dirt.

And just like that, his idea that Sara stay at the Reed house until he returned changed from a suggestion to a demand. He didn't know what was going on here, but it spiked his bodyguard Spidey sense. While he was in Cali-fornia the next day, he'd grab one of his company's state-of-the-art security systems and install it when he returned.

He might've wanted the source of his reawakening emo-tional turmoil to be out of his life, but he sure as hell didn't want any harm to come to her.

Chapter Four

Early Wednesday morning, Nate sat at their round kitchen table and watched Sara tiptoe from the staircase to the front door, where she set her sneakers.

She turned around and tiptoed halfway to the kitchen before she looked up. "Agh!" She froze for a moment, then continued into the room. "You scared the daylights out of me."

Nate chuckled. "You're quite the early bird, aren't you?"

"Looks like you win the worm, though." Sara took a mug from the cupboard, filled it with steaming coffee and joined him at the table. "I thought you weren't due back until this evening."

"I finished my business meetings sooner than planned and caught an earlier flight. I got in late last night." He'd returned from California ahead of time with the intention of getting the window replaced and alarm installed today. That way Sara could move into the mansion on Thursday, and his life could return to normal. Having her under the same roof, a mere twenty feet away as he'd tried to fall asleep the past two nights, was too much of a distraction for him. *Out of sight, out of mind.* "Did you go back over to the house yesterday?"

"No. I spent most of the day touring the justice center with Cassie, checking out my courtroom and cleaning out the desk in my chambers. After four decades as a judge, Harmon had quite the assortment of personal belongings in his drawers. Not to mention petrified food crumbs, dust bunnies and things I'd rather not mention before breakfast." Sara grimaced. "And I ordered a couple of robes, so I'll be ready to take the bench as soon as I'm sworn in."

The front door opened and closed, and Cassie strode into the kitchen, her Western boot heels clomping across the hardwood floors. "Mornin'."

"Not everyone's awake yet, sis." Nate gave her an admonishing look.

"Well, they should be." She eyed the stairs. "Adam needs to handle the department briefing this morning while Sara and I start packing up Harmon's stuff in the mansion." Her lips pursed, as if disappointed that speaking his name didn't make the second-oldest Reed magically appear. She rounded on Nate. "What are *you* doing here?"

"I live here."

"He got back early," Sara added.

Cassie smiled. "Good. You can help us."

Nate shook his head. "Sorry, I'll be installing a full security system over there today."

When Sara frowned at him, he tried to play off his concern. "Best to err on the side of caution." He cringed internally at the cliché, but he didn't want to alarm her.

"We need to get going." Cassie glanced at her watch. "The cleaning crew will be there soon."

"Thank goodness. I can't wait until the dust and dirt are gone from that place." Sara scrunched her nose in a cute way, and Nate decided he liked it when she did that.

He leaned back in his chair and looked at the two women. "Looks like y'all dressed for the job."

Cassie had on worn denim jeans and a T-shirt. Sara wore

a pink shirt tucked into what looked like another pair of designer jeans. Nate almost laughed at the image of a city mouse and a country mouse. But neither of these women were meek little mice. Not by a long shot.

Sara rose and led the way to the front door, where she wriggled her feet into her sneakers without untying them. Nate followed behind Cassie, grabbing his keys on the way out. "I'll stop by that new bakery and grab a box of kolaches on my way over. I should get to the mansion just about the time all the heavy lifting's done." He gave them a Cheshire cat grin when they glanced back at him, all four of their brows raised in a *you'd better be joking* look.

"What?" He was all wide-eyed innocence.

Cassie headed toward her cruiser, raising her hand in an uncharacteristic middle-finger salute. "Make sure at least half are jalapeño sausage with cheese."

"And make sure they're fresh," Sara tossed over her shoulder.

Nate blew out a heavy breath as he closed and locked the front door. Definitely not mice. Whatever the opposite of mice was, that was what those two were.

"This is the last from the dresser." Sara dropped an armload of T-shirts and rolled pairs of socks onto the bed.

While Cassie packed them into an already half-filled box, Sara rechecked every drawer in the room, both wardrobes and took another look under the bed.

"Looks like we're finished in here."

"Good." Cassie taped the box closed. "This wasn't as hard as going through my dad's stuff, but I'm glad we're through."

They found Nate in the dining room downstairs. A large box of pastries and a pile of napkins sat on the end of the dining room table.

"You buy out the store?" Cassie asked as she picked up a rolled sausage kolache with a napkin. She mumbled something else, but it didn't make it around the mouthful.

Nate grabbed an open-faced one with fruit. "I got enough so the cleaning crew can help themselves, too."

Sara shot him a covert glance, impressed that he'd thought about the others who'd be working here today. As his head pivoted toward her, she dropped her eyes and examined the Czech treats, finally choosing a sausage-filled one. "Thank heavens you got coffee, too." Picking up a to-go cup, she sipped the steaming hot brew, striving for the extreme daily allotment of caffeine she was used to.

A knock on the door announced the cleaning crew's arrival. Sara directed two upstairs to start on the main bedroom and bath. Two more headed into the kitchen, and the other three dispersed to rooms downstairs. Meanwhile, Nate began opening the many boxes he'd brought with him.

"All of these are for the alarm system?" Sara asked.

"I've got cameras, glass-breakage monitors, the alarm panel, backup battery—all kinds of good stuff." Nate smiled up at her, and her mind shut down for a second.

Cassie cocked her head, eying her brother. "Don't you need a Texas license before you can install a security system *in* Texas?"

"Cool your jets, sis. I've got a licensed friend coming by to do the wiring. He'll make sure we're legal."

One of the women working in the kitchen appeared in the dining room doorway. "There's a broken window in the utility room."

Nate continued to unbox cameras. "I boarded it up the other day. The glass guy should be here soon to replace it."

"There's no board over it now." The woman seemed unsettled, her hands wrapped around each other as if she was washing them. "And I guess you've already seen the graffiti on the wall in there?"

"What graffiti?" Sara managed around the small bite of food in her mouth. She headed for the room behind the kitchen.

As she read the message written in garish red spray paint on one of the walls, the blood drained from her head and pooled in her feet. This wasn't the work of ball-playing juveniles. This was from the creep who'd been texting her.

told you id find you

Sara raised one hand to her mouth, her skin icy to the touch.

"The hell?" Nate spent more time studying Sara than the wall. "You look like you've seen the grim reaper."

"What's going on, Sara?" Cassie snapped pictures of the graffiti and empty window opening with her phone. "Do you know who did this?"

Shaking her head, Sara turned and trudged back to the dining room. Cassie dispersed the cleaning crew to other rooms before she and Nate followed.

"I've been getting some weird texts for a while now." Sara fished her phone out of her pocket. "I figured they were just wrong numbers."

"What's weird about them?" Nate asked.

"Up until this week they weren't threatening, they just gave me the creeps." Sara scrolled through her texts. "But Monday I got this one shortly after arriving at your house."

She read the last text out loud: "'You can run, but you can't hide. I'll find you.'"

Cassie held out her hand for Sara's phone. "Have you replied to any of them?"

"No. I didn't want to engage with whoever's sending them. I was afraid even if it was a wrong number, replying might encourage them." She passed her phone to her friend. "I've tried blocking the numbers, but I didn't delete any of them."

Cassie handed the phone to Nate after she'd read all the texts. "We need to arrange security for you. I can make sure one of my deputies is with you at all times. And maybe you should just stay at the ranch instead of—"

"No. I'm not going to run scared, and I refuse to disrupt your family's lives by hiding out in their house. Uniformed deputies attached to me by the hip will only draw more attention. I haven't even been sworn in yet. The county commissioners would probably suggest you send me packing and find another judge."

Cassie crossed her arms over her chest. "As the local sheriff, it's my responsibility to protect the judge of Boone Co—"

"No, Cassie." She planted her hands on her hips. "I don't want to start out on the wrong foot with the whole county. I'll be fine with Nate's alarm system."

Her friend's eyes narrowed, and Sara couldn't tell which way she was going to lean. Finally, Cassie gave a short nod. "Fine. But I *am* going to file a report so we've got a record of this." She jabbed a finger in Sara's direction. "But if anything else happens, I'm doing what I think best."

Sara nodded back, though at the moment she doubted her agreement mattered to her friend, the quintessential sheriff.

"Your swearing in is Monday. Between now and then, you need to rack your brain for possible suspects. People you prosecuted who went to prison, anyone you know personally who may have a grudge against you, ex-boyfriends whose hearts you broke… I don't care how unimportant they may seem."

Still reading Sara's texts, Nate's gaze jerked up at Cassie's words.

Sara nodded her agreement. "I haven't been able to think of anyone so far, but I'll keep trying."

"Good. And I want you to stay at the ranch until we find whoever's doing this." Cassie took Sara's phone from Nate and gave it back to her.

"I appreciate the offer, but I don't want to impose any longer than necessary. I'm moving in tomorrow so I can get settled and be ready to hit the ground running next week." Sara stood. "End of conversation."

Without taking sides in the discussion, Nate went back to opening boxes. "While my buddy gets this system wired in, I'll go pick up a can of paint to cover the graffiti."

"Thank you. I'd prefer not to look at it every time I walk in there." Sara already felt safer because of all Nate was doing to help her.

"I'm finished packing Judge Harmon's stuff." Cassie picked up one of the boxes they'd brought down from upstairs. "Let's get these in my car. I'll have Helen ship them to his family."

As Nate shoved the last box into the back of the SUV and closed the rear door, Cassie approached Sara with a newspaper in hand.

"I almost forgot to show this to you. You made the front page." Cassie grinned as she held the paper open. "It's just the *Boone County Register*, but I checked online and several other newspapers picked it up. Including the one in Austin."

Sara skimmed the article, naming her as the new county judge. It included a brief biography of her, mentioning her stint as an Austin assistant district attorney. She loved the idea that her ex-boss, who always read the digital edition of the Austin paper, would see this article.

Do you miss me now, Alton?

But as Nate read over her shoulder, another thought occurred to her. She glanced at the top of the page. Sunday's edition. "I wonder if this is how he found out where I am." She met Cassie's eyes and watched as realization dawned.

"It might be. Dadgummit! I should've thought of that."

"Just because you're the sheriff doesn't mean you can connect two completely unrelated things at the drop of a hat. Plus, you just found out about the texts." Sara gave her friend a warm smile. "And I haven't heard that word in way too long."

All three laughed at Cassie's aversion to hardcore swearing.

"Listen, call me immediately if you get another text, okay?"

"I will." The immediate shock from the graffiti had worn off. Sara was certain, between Nate's alarm system and her best friends in town being law enforcement officers, that whoever was bothering her would disappear back beneath the rock they'd crawled out from under.

"And Nate, you don't have to leave town for good until December, right?"

"Yeah?" He drew the word out as if he knew he wouldn't like Cassie's reason for asking.

"Good. Since Sara refuses to stay at the ranch, I want *you* to stay with *her*."

Nate stared at his sister as if her words made no sense, and Sara's gaze bounced between the two.

Cassie twisted her mouth to the side. "You're a bodyguard, right?"

"Yeah, but—"

Poking a finger into her brother's chest to accentuate her words, Cassie said, "I'll have Helen set you up as an approved vendor for the county, with authorized expenses. Because as of this moment, you're officially guarding Sara's body."

"Oh, I don't think that's necessary." Sara's cheeks warmed with embarrassment.

Cassie waved her hand in the air. "Y'all know how I meant that. And yes, Sara, it *is* necessary. You don't want deputies in uniform hanging around? Then you get my brother, the bodyguard."

After Nate made a few false starts with a reply, Cassie planted her fists on her hips and leaned toward him. "Do you *not* think she could be in danger? Do you *not* think she'd be a heck of a lot safer with you protecting her?" She turned her head slightly and gave him the side-eye. "Do you *not* want to do me this favor that will put me in your debt?"

When Nate agreed to do Cassie's bidding, Sara withered on the inside. One of the main reasons she hadn't wanted to stay at the ranch was to avoid Nate. Now she'd be sharing quarters with him. A man with a life waiting for him in California. A man she still found hard to resist. Not for the first time, Sara wondered exactly what she'd gotten herself into.

"OF COURSE, CASSIE." Nate muttered under his breath as he attached a motion-activated light beneath an eave. "Anything for you, Cassie."

He'd been reluctant to become Sara's bodyguard, and with good reason. He couldn't miss the California meeting for the contract he'd worked so hard to land. And then there was the bruised-ego thing from when the older, sophisticated college girl had stolen his heart, then forgotten about him when she left town. But the Reeds always had each other's backs, so for Cassie's sake, he'd grudgingly agreed.

What really stuck in his craw was that his sister was right. Sara *could* be in real danger, and she *would* be safer with him providing personal security. His main objective until now had been to keep as much distance as possible between him and the woman Sara had become. To stop wondering if her lips still tasted as sweet, if the scent of her skin would still drive him crazy.

But the graffiti upped the ante. In the past, he'd protected an array of clients, and he'd always kept it professional. Holding in his temper when guarding some loathsome billionaire who'd considered him nothing more than a hired gun. Keeping his fly zipped when semi-famous starlets had tried to lure him into their beds.

With his integrity on the line, Nate was always able to set aside his personal opinions—as well as ignore momentary temptations—in order to do the job. Regardless of everything else, leaving someone in the path of peril when he could protect them went against his core beliefs. He'd do the same with Sara. But God help him, his sister had no idea what she'd asked him to do.

"Nate?" Blake, the Texas-licensed alarm installer, stood next to the ladder.

Nate looked down at his friend. "Yeah?"

"Two questions. You want the main control panel in the attic? And how many keypads and where?"

"If the attic picks up a strong-enough signal, then it will work. Otherwise, wherever you think best." Nate shielded his eyes from the late afternoon sun's glare with one hand. "Keypads by the front and back doors, and one in the master bedroom."

"Got it." Blake looked at a paper in his hand. "You sure

you want glass sensors by *every* window on the ground floor? The alarm will go off if any of them are opened."

"Yeah, but it won't if someone breaks the glass. There's a box in the dining room with more than enough of them."

Blake scoffed. "Hey, I'm not arguing. You're the one paying for my time." He disappeared around a corner of the house.

Over the past year, Nate had tried a few times to convince Blake to move out to California and work for Reed & Franklin Security. Alarm installations had picked up as crime increased, and his friend was one of the best. But Blake had no desire to leave Texas.

By dinnertime, the window was replaced, the entire alarm system was working and the graffiti was hidden behind two coats of primer. Sara walked into the sparkling-clean kitchen as Nate crouched over the paint can and pounded its lid on.

"Where have you been hiding?" He looked up at her dirt-smudged face.

"I found the door to the attic stairs and went exploring. Even with all the weird stuff taking up space, I'll have plenty of room to move some of the old furniture up there if I decide I just can't live with them. I'm assuming, since they don't belong to me, I can't donate them to a charity. Or a museum." She rolled her eyes, then gave the wall a critical once-over. "I thought you were going to paint it white, not just prime it."

Nate followed her gaze as he stood. "Even though white's the best choice, Cassie said you might want to pick out your own color."

"Really?" Sara beamed. "We get to pick out paint chips?"

"Well, I was thinking *you* could, but since I'll be your shadow for the duration, I guess *we'll* get to." He stepped closer and rubbed his thumb across a black streak on her cheek. "I think the point of bringing in a cleaning crew was so you wouldn't have to."

"Oh." Her grimy cheeks blushed, and she covered them with her hands. "I felt useless sitting around, and I didn't mind helping. But I must be a mess."

She didn't look like a mess. Even covered in dust and dirt, Sara was beautiful. But saying that out loud would blur the line between professional and personal conduct. "You look fine." He checked the clock on the wall. "We better get to gettin'. Adam will have dinner on the table soon."

"Give me a minute. I can't leave looking like this." Sara opened drawers until she found kitchen towels, then held one under the faucet. After scrubbing her face with it, she asked, "Better?"

Nate took the towel from her. "You missed a few spots." Stepping closer, he wiped gently at a speck of dirt on her temple. Her eyelids closed as he tipped her chin up to get at the streak along her jawline.

While he cleaned away a grimy dot on the tip of her small, straight nose, the smattering of freckles across it fascinated him. He paused, and she opened her eyes. They were a light blue, more inviting than pictures he'd seen of the Caribbean Sea. Forcing his feet back a step, Nate willed away the heat building inside of him.

But holding back would take a will of iron. Even though he'd had some difficult, dangerous jobs in the past, this one would definitely win the blue ribbon in Assignments Best Not Taken.

Chapter Five

Friday morning, Sara turned off her alarm and luxuriated in the new king-size bed she'd ordered online earlier in the week. No matter how short a time she'd be in Resolute, she refused to sleep in a small bed with a saggy mattress. Adding a set of sheets had been a good move, since she definitely wouldn't use the old sheets and pillowcases already in the house.

Nate hadn't seemed to mind the furniture in his room. He'd chosen the one closest to hers. For security reasons, he'd said. Didn't mean she hadn't spent far too much time attaching far too much meaning to the choice.

Speaking of security, he'd turned the breakfast room into command central. A folding table had been added to hold multiple monitors. Several showed live-action footage from four cameras each. One large screen showed what was happening as seen from *all* the cameras, and a few more were set up to zoom in on one zone at a time.

It all seemed a bit much for a few creepy texts and one wall of graffiti. Then she remembered how unsettled she'd felt and was secretly glad for the overkill. One thing was certain—she wouldn't be wandering around the backyard in her pajamas anytime soon.

After stretching and yawning for a few minutes, she

zipped through her morning bathroom routine, got dressed and headed downstairs. The scent of coffee drew her to the kitchen, where she poured herself a cup from a percolator.

"That's the only thing I could find to make coffee in." Nate stood in the entrance to the breakfast room. "You might want to add a coffee maker to your shopping list."

Sara managed to swallow a small sip before dumping the bitter brew into the sink. She should have brought hers along from Austin. But when she'd heard the word *mansion*, she assumed there'd at least be a decent coffee machine. "Already on there." She was looking forward to today's trip to Victoria. Along with the espresso machine and more sheet sets, she had a long list of other essentials—at least, essential for her—that the mansion lacked. Not to mention a second list of groceries that she doubted the local store carried.

"You ready to go?" Nate set his cup in the sink.

"I am if there's a fast-food joint on the way. I'm not used to starting out my day with no caffeine." After pulling on her jacket to ward off the early morning chill, she grabbed her keys from the long console table in the foyer.

"There is, and you don't need your keys. I'm driving."

"Look, I appreciate you protecting me, but I'm perfectly capable of driving." Sara raised her brows. "Or does it threaten your masculine ego to ride shotgun while a woman drives?"

Apparently not to be outdone, Nate's single brow arch gave off a tuxedoed super-spy vibe. "My masculine ego thrives when I'm in a passenger seat. It leaves my hands free for other things."

Her gaze dropped to his hands, her mind picturing his arm lying across the center console, his fingers on her right thigh. She cursed her fair skin when her cheeks started to burn.

"But not when I'm on duty. I don't question your ability behind the wheel, but if the need arises for evasive driving, I doubt you'll match my skill."

"Fine." She set the keys down. She was irritated by him calling the shots, aggravated by her brief but sensual imagining and extreme caffeine deprivation. When her stomach growled, she settled on hangry. "But I need food and coffee. Now."

A smile toyed at the corners of Nate's mouth, which irritated her even more, and when he opened the door Sara breezed past him.

He escorted her to the garage, where he'd parked his truck. Her vehicle was parked in the street due to a single-car driveway and, as Nate had explained it, so no one could tamper with his—nothing personal. "After I open the door, wait for me to clear it before you go in."

The garage doors were locked, and the building had no windows. Using her abilities learned during court trials, she waited patiently without rolling her eyes or heaving heavy sighs. From an early age, Sara had been in control of her own life. Apparently Nate had become a bit of a control addict himself—at least, when he was working security.

With the graffiti gone and the alarm system installed, her fear had dissipated. But if Nate insisted on playing bodyguard and shadowing her every step, fine. She'd see how much he enjoyed her day-long shopping extravaganza. He wouldn't know what hit him.

NATE RELAXED BACK against the vinyl booth seat and exhaled while Sara gave the Busy B Café's menu a quick look. Then she picked up her phone, and her thumbs hadn't stopped moving since.

"Something urgent?" Raised in a family of law enforcement officers, he was used to phones being answered dur-ing meals. But her phone hadn't rung, and he was starting to feel ignored.

Without lifting her eyes, Sara replied, "Hmm?"

He had to hand it to her, her focus was impressive. A glance at his watch told Nate they'd shopped for seven hours straight and hadn't even made it to the grocery store. With nothing to cook at the mansion, Sara had insisted they eat here before hauling home her truckload of purchases. She was just lucky he had a crew-cab pickup. Leaving expen-sive stuff in an open truck bed while shopping for more expensive stuff was never a good idea.

Marge, owner of the Busy B and gossiper extraordi-naire, set two mugs on the table. "You kids want coffee?" She smiled knowingly at his slumped posture against the booth seat. "Looks like *you* need some, Nate."

He nodded. "Marge, this is Sara Bennett, our new county judge. Sara, Marge here—"

Sara finally looked up from her phone. "Marge!" She stood from the bench seat in one smooth move and hugged the older woman. "It's so good to see you again."

"You too, honey." Marge set the coffee carafe down and took hold of Sara's shoulders, giving her a once-over. "You look fit as a fiddle in a bluegrass band. I heard you were comin' to town on a temporary-permanent basis."

Nate filled his mug from the carafe. "And I guess you two already know each other."

Both women looked at him as if he'd had two heads.

"Of course we know each other." Marge scoffed. "Cassie brought Sara in here years ago when she came to visit y'all."

"And I made sure to stop by for one of Marge's magic milkshakes when I was in town this past summer for the youth center grand opening." Sara gave Marge another hug before she slid back onto her seat. "Highlight of my trip."

Marge beamed as she picked up the carafe. "So what'll it be tonight? Coffee or a milkshake?"

"Umm…" Sara glanced back at the menu.

Nate piped up. "I'll have a double cheeseburger with fries. And the coffee."

"That sounds good. I'll have the same, but just a single. Fries and a chocolate shake."

"Comin' right up. I'll send over a couple waters, too." Marge winked at Sara as she picked up the menus. "Seein' as my shakes are so thick, you can hold 'em upside down without a drop hittin' the tabletop." Her laugh accompanied the squeak of her orthopedic shoes on the linoleum floor as she headed for the kitchen.

"I could've kept shopping until the stores closed if I hadn't gotten so hungry." Sara studied Nate, her lips twitching. "But you look exhausted."

Hoping the steam from his coffee was infused with caffeine, Nate inhaled it as he stared at her over his mug. "Can't imagine why."

Sara Bennett would own a gold medal if shopping ever became a competitive sport. First, they'd gone to the free-standing stores that carried linens, small kitchen appliances, electronics and items to organize all the other stuff she'd bought or was about to. While she had pointed to or handed him items, he ferried them to the cart, which she'd left for him to push. Just in case he needed to practice his evasive maneuvers, she'd told him.

Then they'd gone to the mall. Who knew one place could have so many shoe stores? Granted, she did need more appropriate footwear for country living, and her sensible choice of work boots that would stave off a rattler's fangs, along with a fashionable pair of Western boots that didn't scream *city slicker*, impressed him. But only the threat of accompanying her into the dressing room—for her own safety, of course—had put the kibosh on clothes shopping.

"Need a top-off?" April, the newest server in the diner, stood ready with a fresh pot of coffee and a shy smile. Marge had hired her after Rachel, Adam's fiancée, quit to work full-time with the county youth program. She was young and, according to Marge, had a huge crush on Nate.

"Please." He pushed his mug closer to her and gave her a friendly smile.

When the server reached for Sara's mug with her brows raised in question, Sara held her hand over it. "I appreciate you offering, but I'm waiting for one of the best chocolate milkshakes in the world."

April nodded. "OMG. Aren't they the most delicious things you ever tasted? We get to eat for free after our shifts, and I *always* get a milkshake." Her grin was almost too big for her face. "Just a milkshake." As she spoke, her gaze kept drifting to Nate.

"Now you're just making me jealous." Sara grinned back. Once April moved on to the next table, Sara shifted her gaze to him, her smile now smug.

"What?"

"I think she likes you."

"Who likes him?" Marge set their plates on the table.

"The waitress who just stopped by." Sara aimed her little twisted grin at the older woman.

Marge took a quick look around the room. "April? Oh, sure—I've told him that." She placed a milkshake in front of Sara, then glared at Nate. "And I've also told him I won't allow any cradle robbing of my employees."

Nate dropped the french fry he was holding onto his plate

and met Marge's eyes. "And I've told Marge I have no interest in her employees."

"Then reserve that thousand-watt smile and dimples-to-die-for for someone you *are* interested in." Marge let out an exaggerated sigh. "I swear, every time that girl waits on you, her mind disappears for the rest of the day."

Nate pressed both hands to his chest. "How is this all *my* fault?"

"Nate's right, Marge. He can't help it that he's so darn adorable." Sara unwrapped her straw. "And to be honest, he didn't even look at her."

"Well, that's a good thing. Keep it that way." She turned and winked at Nate, then headed toward the front counter.

Sara frowned. "I don't know Marge very well, but I can't believe she thinks you'd flirt with someone that young."

"She doesn't." Nate chuckled. "Marge is Cassie's adviser, Adam's biggest fan and Noah's defender when it comes to his antics. Me, she likes to tease. As soon as she noticed April's interest in me, it became her latest favorite topic."

"How old do you think she is?" Sara sucked milkshake through her straw.

"April?" He shrugged. "I don't know. I'd guess eighteen, nineteen." He took a bite of burger and chewed while Sara looked up at him from beneath hooded eyes, still sucking on her shake.

She was probably getting at something to do with age and…flirting and maybe something else, but for the life of him he couldn't concentrate enough to figure it out. Her pursed lips surrounded the tip of the straw that she held between her thumb and first two fingers. And with each draw, her cheeks disappeared inward. He shifted slightly on the bench, watching her throat work as she swallowed.

Then, apparently oblivious to the effect she'd just had

on him, she said, "So, about the same age you were when I met you." Her brows pulled together in a troubled frown.

"There's a hell of a difference between three years and ten or eleven years." Nate set his burger down and wiped his hands on a napkin. "Is that why you ghosted me after spring break? You thought you were *robbing the cradle*?"

Sara glanced past his shoulder. "Let's discuss this another time."

An elderly man stopped at their table and after a small nod toward Nate, turned to Sara. "Excuse me for interrupting your meal, but are you our new judge?"

"Yes, I'm Sara Bennett." She reached out to shake hands. "It's nice to meet you, Mr…?"

He pumped her hand. "Dodson. Fred Dodson."

"Nice to meet you, Mr. Dodson."

"Please, call me Fred." As Sara eased her hand out of his, he continued. "I must say, you're a sight easier on the eyes than old Harmon was." Still leaning toward her, Frank winked. "I hope we'll see you at the weekly church pancake breakfasts. We've got an open seat for you at the mayor's table."

"Thank you very much. I'll need to check my schedule." Patting her stomach, she added, "And I'm afraid I wouldn't fit behind the bench if I indulged *every* week." Sara chuckled, and the old man ate it up.

"Aw, hell, if Harmon could fit back there, ten of you could." Frank laughed. "Well, I better let y'all get back to your dinner. And I'll look forward to seeing *you*—" he pointed at her "—at breakfast." He shuffled back in the direction he'd appeared from.

"Talk about robbing the cradle," Nate muttered, and Sara choked back her laughter until Fred was out of earshot. When it finally broke loose, Nate joined her.

He'd assumed the town wouldn't be receptive to a citified female judge after almost a half century with a good ol' boy on the bench. But it was impressive how well Sara was already managing to connect with the locals. Marge, April and Fred Dodson loved her. All of his siblings loved her.

Now Nate's only problem, besides keeping her safe, was to avoid downing the Sara-Bennett-love-potion drink mix. Because Lord knew it would be a disaster to fall in love with her. Again.

DURING THE DRIVE home from the diner, Sara refused to let Nate's silence dampen her mood. "I can't believe I got everything on my shopping list today."

"Except food." His droll tone made her chuckle.

"We can zip back over to Victoria tomorrow morning and take care of that." She pulled her phone out of her purse. "I don't suppose there are any grocery stores that deliver to Resolute."

Nate looked at her with a blank expression. "From Victoria?" He scoffed. "You sure you can survive here for a few months?"

She rolled her eyes. "Like you don't enjoy *your* creature comforts when you're in California? Yet you seem to transition pretty smoothly from expensive suits to jeans and T-shirts."

The truck bumped over the edge of the driveway, and Nate shifted into Park but left the engine idling. He shifted sideways to face her. "I don't wear expensive suits unless I have to. And how would you know what I wear in California?"

For someone who spoke with precision in a courtroom, every word weighed and measured before it left her mouth, Sara couldn't seem to keep her foot out of said mouth when it came to small talk with Nate.

"I must have seen a picture of you on Cassie's phone." She tried to pass the fib off with a shrug. "Not that it matters." She crossed her arms when his eyes narrowed. "My point is I'd wager I can adapt to my environment just as well as you can."

Nate held her gaze a moment longer, then opened his door. "Stay in the truck until we're parked inside." He climbed out, surveyed the front yard, then unlocked and opened the garage.

Even with the embarrassment from her verbal blunder, followed closely with aggravation at being ordered around by him on *her* temporary property, Sara couldn't pull her eyes away from Nate. The muscles across his broad back flexed and stretched as he lifted the heavy door, and unbidden memories surfaced. Memories she'd tried to erase for years.

Nate got back into the truck and eased it forward into the garage. Sara jumped out the second the engine cut off and grabbed a few bags from the back seat. As she strode toward the house, he rushed to keep up.

"You can't just take off like that." He unlocked the front door, ushered her inside and disarmed the alarm. "Stay here while I clear the house."

"Seriously? Wouldn't the alarm have gone off if anyone broke in?" Sara continued into the dining room, where she set her purchases on the table.

"Damn it!" Nate did a quick walk-through of the downstairs before returning to her. "You *have* to do what I say if you expect me to keep you safe."

About to vent her frustration, Sara realized she was going about this all wrong. "You're right. I'm sorry." She headed for the front door.

"Where do you think you're going?" His long legs got him there before her.

"To get my stuff out of your truck."

"No. You stay inside, where I know you're safe." Nate, obviously thinking he had the upper hand, smiled at her sudden cooperation. "I'll bring in the rest."

Sara nodded in agreement, and while Nate carried in load after load of bags and boxes, she remained at the long table, unpacking everything.

"Did you have to buy the biggest, most expensive coffee-and-espresso machine in the store?" he asked as he walked into the kitchen.

"You'll thank me tomorrow morning."

"You're going to contaminate that shiny new toy with our old, stale coffee?" He trudged past her for the umpteenth time.

Sara glanced up from the new towels she was sorting into stacks. "Darn, that's right—I've got fresh coffee on my grocery list. Oh, well. You'll thank me *Sunday* morning."

"Whatever you say," he muttered.

Who's following whose orders now?

A few minutes later, the garage door closed with a thump, and Nate delivered the last of her purchases to her. He disappeared into the kitchen, then returned with a flashlight. "Back in a minute. I just need to check something."

Finally ready to acknowledge her exhaustion, Sara collapsed onto a chair as the front door opened and closed. She should've felt guilty about making Nate do so much of the heavy lifting, but this whole protection thing seemed more unnecessary by the day. She hadn't even gotten a text since the one on Monday. And having to answer to someone constantly, especially in her personal life, got her hackles up.

The door opened and closed again, the alarm panel buttons beeped and Nate's quick footsteps carried him into the room. "We need to go upstairs."

"I'll wait here if you feel a need to *clear* the second floor. I'm bushed."

"*Now*, Sara." He rounded the table and pulled her into a standing position. "I want to check the security footage."

"Why?" The bold confidence in her belief she was safe left her like the air in a popped balloon. "What's wrong?" She allowed Nate to grab her hand and lead her up the stairs.

"Someone slashed all four of your tires."

Chapter Six

"All rise!"

Tuesday morning, Nate was standing in the judge's doorway, watching Sara enter the courtroom, her blond hair shining in the light pouring down from the high windows. After driving back to Victoria on Saturday morning for groceries, they'd hunkered down in the house for the rest of the weekend, careful to stay out of each other's way.

"Boone County Court is now in session. The Honorable Judge Bennett is presiding." The bailiff looked out over a packed gallery of gawkers, her stern voice at odds with the general atmosphere of curiosity and comical anticipation. The spectators, not just from Resolute but the entire county, were here to see the new judge in action as well as watch a trial about geese.

Sara took her seat, and the bailiff finished with, "Be seated."

Nate slipped in and took up a position off to the side of the bench. A perfect spot to see the entire room and still be close enough to protect Sara if the stalker tried to get to her.

The attorneys approached the bench to speak quietly with Sara, and Nate scanned the room, studying every face, searching for furtive movements. His eyes still burned from the long hours on his computer over the weekend, investigating Sara Bennett. She didn't have social media accounts—most likely a smart move for a prosecutor. But inmates with contraband cell phones managed to post in various places, and the comments he'd found about Sara made his fingers curl into a fist.

For some reason, his usual ability to compartmentalize work and his personal life was failing him. He'd like to blame it on exhaustion, but Sara was right—the new espresso machine was amazing, and he'd spent the past weekend running searches on a full tank of caffeine.

During breaks from his research, he'd reviewed recorded footage from the property. The only item of interest so far had been the short, stocky person on foot approaching Sara's car shortly after they'd left to go shopping. But the guy had successfully hidden his identity by wearing a hoodie pulled over his head, and with no other houses on that block, he didn't have to worry about explaining the ski mask that covered his face.

And whenever Nate gave his eyes a break from the monitors, he had spent the time calling Cassie and Adam. Requesting arrest and court records for everyone Sara had prosecuted took time and resources he didn't have.

"Bailiff, please bring in the plaintiff and defendants." Sara's clear voice, sharper and louder than the one she used when off the clock, silenced the murmurs filling the room.

What would normally have been the jury's entrance was opened for Abby Parsons and Ray and Ruth McNulty. Apparently the court personnel had to switch things up due to the crowd in the hallway still trying to get a seat.

Nate didn't know a lot about judges trying civil cases, but he figured there had to be a learning curve. Sara had no experience in that and hadn't had much time yet to study up on it. He hoped today was a success for her, even while keeping his expectations low. And those expectations bottomed out when the McNultys entered the courtroom, each leading a goose by a short red leash.

His gaze shot from the geese to Sara, and he rolled his lips between his teeth to keep from laughing out loud. She managed to cover her mouth with a finger as if in deep thought, but her wide eyes gave away her shock. While the defendants took their seats, she shot Nate a sideways glance. All he could do was smile.

One corner of her mouth twitched behind her finger.

Abby Parsons's lawyer began his opening statement. It seemed this case dealt directly with the situation involving Noah and his then partner, now fiancée, Bree, from earlier this year. Their call out to the McNultys about a trespasser held at bay by a gaggle of geese had been Bree's first experience with the ornery birds. It was a hilarious story Noah still enjoyed teasing her about.

But the disclosure about the Widow Parson's affair with Ray McNulty didn't come out until the defense attorney's statement. The spectators, most of whom already knew about the extra-marital relationship, still oohed and aahed as the juicier details were revealed. They'd come to watch the new judge, but two live geese and adultery now held their attention.

Taking the stand, Abby vowed to tell the truth before launching into a fabricated version of the day Ruth's geese had attacked her. The room filled with giggles and snorts as she described Ruth McNulty leading her gaggle of geese in an assault on the poor, defenseless widow. "And what's more, I did *not* have an affair with Ray McNulty."

Even if Nate hadn't heard the goose story directly from Noah, Ray and Abby's affair was public knowledge around Resolute.

As Abby began recounting all her alleged injuries, Sara said, "Thank you, Mrs. Parsons. I've already reviewed the list you submitted through your attorney. If there's no other *new* testimony, I'll hear from the defendants now."

Abby rose. "I'm sure if Judge Harmon was still here, he'd be much more interested in *my* side of the story."

"That may be, Mrs. Parsons. Then again, I've heard Judge Harmon was a stickler about perjury and procedures." Sara lifted a brow toward the geese. "It seems we're playing a little fast and loose on both today."

Nate mentally applauded her, and based on the nodding heads and murmurs, it looked like quite a few others were as well.

Cassie slipped into the courtroom and stood against the back wall. When she asked *How's it going?* by raising her brows, he gave her a thumbs-up.

Ruth McNulty now sat in the witness box, one of the geese on her lap.

"Is that one of the geese that allegedly attacked the plaintiff?" her lawyer asked.

"Yes. This is Greta."

"Why do you have her with you today?" The attorney kept his distance.

"To show that my geese aren't aggressive unless they're being threatened or they're protecting me." She ran her hand across Greta's back. "The only reason they chased that bi—"

"Mrs. McNulty." Sara's loud interruption caused the goose to twist its neck and stare at her. "Watch your language in my courtroom."

"Sorry, Your Honor." Ruth ducked her head, the picture of contrite. "The only reason my babies chased Mrs. Parsons was because she'd trespassed onto my property. They're kinda like guard dogs. They know who belongs there and who don't, and *she*—" Ruth pointed at Abby "—don't." Her venomous glare was far more convincing than her apologetic expression just seconds earlier.

Abby glared right back.

"That harlot was trying to meet Ray for a *sexual rendezvous* when my geese just did what they're supposed to do," Ruth continued, skirting the edge of profanity. "Protect me from nasty predators trying to get their hands on what's *mine*."

Abby stood, hands on hips. "She's the one who sent me the message to come over, pretending to be Ray." She stomped one high heel on the hardwood floor. "That's entrapment, you old windbag."

Greta hissed and slipped off of Ruth's lap, loose leash trailing behind her. Before the bailiff could reach the bird, it took off at a waddle-sprint toward Abby, its wings spread wide. Abby's high-pitched shriek echoed through the courtroom as she clambered up onto the attorney's table. Ray's goose yanked loose from his tether and headed down the center aisle, hissing at spectators. When one woman jumped up and ran for the door, the goose pumped its head up and down, then took chase.

Chaos erupted.

"Good grief." Nate kept his eyes trained on Sara, not liking the sudden bedlam and what it meant for his ability to protect her if needed.

He watched as Sara picked up her gavel, ready to bang it for the very first time. Probably something every judge remembered for the rest of their life.

But when she pounded the gavel on its base, it exploded in a cloud of smoke and sparks. Nate raced toward the bench, vaulting the witness stand to tackle Sara to the floor and cover her with his body.

"Are you all right?" His hands patted down her robe, searching for hot sparks. "Were you burned?" Satisfied she was unharmed, he stopped his body search and looked into her fear-filled eyes.

Her lips parted and closed a few times, but she seemed unable to speak.

A few minutes later, Cassie crouched down next to them. "Nate, is she okay?"

Sara's frozen gaze shifted toward her friend. "Isn't this how the last judge died?"

"Not exactly." Nate shifted to his knees and pulled Sara into a sitting position. "What the hell happened, Cass?"

"It looks like some sort of chemical was applied to the gavel. Or its base. Or both." Cassie's nostrils flared, and Nate knew she was mentally berating herself for this happening to her friend under her watch.

So was Nate.

"Noah's collecting all the pieces in an evidence bag. We'll have Forensics examine them, identify the substances." Cassie stood. "I had the bailiff clear the room and I told the McNultys and Ms. Parsons that you'll reschedule their trial, but no geese allowed next time."

Cassie nodded.

"Nate, we'll wrap up things here while you get Sara home." Tracking everyone's movements, she didn't look at him when she asked, "You want a deputy to accompany you?"

"Couldn't hurt." He wrapped his arms around Sara and lifted her to her feet.

Cassie nodded and headed back toward the almost empty gallery.

Nate, arms still around Sara, walked her into the judge's chambers and closed the door. She leaned against him, her body trembling.

Why is my *heart racing?*

He'd been in shoot-outs, run off roads and chased by a pack of man-eating dogs with a lower pulse rate. The only variance in this situation was Sara.

"You're in shock." He steered her toward a chair. "You should probably sit—"

"I don't want to sit down." Sara stepped out of his arms. "And I'm *not* in shock. I'm furious!"

Nate expelled a heavy breath. "I cleared that courtroom, but I didn't pick up the gavel. I should have, and I'm sorry."

"If you had, you might've been seriously hurt." Sara's eyes softened. "I'm glad you didn't."

"But that's my job. I promise, I'll get to the bottom of this."

"*You* will?" Sara's eyes morphed back into icy blue glaciers. "This was *my* moment, my first time on the bench, damn it. And some sick jerk with an unknown vendetta ruined it. And if that wasn't enough, that was my grandfather's gavel he blew up. Pops gave it to me when he retired as a symbol of his faith in me, in my plan to become a judge someday." Her eyes filled with tears, but she blinked them away. "I'm going to find that sorry excuse for a human being, and when I do, he won't know what hit him."

And apparently I still suck at reading women's emotions.

Sara began unbuttoning her robe.

Nate gestured toward it. "At least that didn't catch fire."

"And do you know why?" She arched a brow, a satisfied smile playing on her lips. "Because this tropical wool material—" she shrugged out of the robe and held it toward him "—that you thought was ridiculously expensive is not only comfortable in any climate but also flame retardant. Unlike that cheap polyester one you suggested."

If there was one thing Nate had learned during his short-term relationships with women, it was when to keep his mouth shut.

"I need to splash some cold water on my face, then I'm ready to go."

"Wait!" Nate strode past her, chastising himself for not having cleared the restroom the minute they'd entered her chambers. He pushed the door open, flipped on the light and froze.

The message he saw in the mirror had been written on the wall next to the door. He tried to fill the doorway so Sara wouldn't see it, but it was too late.

"Nate?" She was right behind him, trying to shove him out of the way. "What is that?"

He stepped into the restroom so she could get past him, then they both stared at the wall. This message looked like it had been written by a finger dipped in red paint, but the metallic scent told Nate it was blood. The fact it wasn't dry yet meant they'd missed the stalker by minutes, if not seconds.

still got all your fingers?

Chapter Seven

"You ready to roll?" Sara handed Nate a cup of coffee when he walked into the kitchen. Having just finished her first week as a judge, she was more than ready to spend the weekend whittling down her to-do list.

Nate scrubbed his fingers through his hair, leaving tufts sticking out in every direction. "*More* shopping? Every day after court, we've run by the hardware store or general store to pick up something else for your master plan to make over the house. What else could you possibly need?"

"I'll show you." She took hold of his shoulders, turned him about-face and nudged him across the hall to the dining room.

Nate walked along the table, taking stock of all the small sample cans, paint swatches and assorted supplies. Large gallons of paint sat on the floor along the wall. "Let me guess—you changed your mind on the colors and want more samples."

"Not yet." Sara waited for him to turn around, then thrust her hand out from behind her back, holding a paint roller. "This is for you. Get it? Ready to roll?" She snickered.

Nate lowered himself onto a chair and set his coffee mug on the table. "You're really going to put to me to work on a Saturday? There's a hockey game I was planning to watch."

Sara folded her arms across her chest. "If I have to stay cooped up in this house indefinitely, except for being chauffeured back and forth to the courthouse, I intend to fix it up to my liking. And if you're going to stay in this house to protect me, you're darn right I'm putting you to work."

After glaring at her for a moment, Nate's shoulders sagged in resignation even while the set of his jaw remained mutinous. "Fine, but I'm having breakfast first."

"That's a good idea." Hiding her satisfied grin, she added, "We both should start the day well-fueled. I'll have whatever you're having."

He didn't utter a word, but as he passed her on his way to the kitchen, his comical side-eye said it all.

"Thank you," she called after him in a sweet voice.

He mumbled something she didn't catch, and she decided it was best that way.

An hour later, plastic lay across the kitchen appliances and counters, tape covered the natural-wood moldings, and Nate was indeed rolling. He stepped back from the wall and tipped his head to the side. "I still think we should just paint it white."

"White's boring. A kitchen should be happy and cheerful." Sara stepped back from the wall she was working on, admiring the pale yellow.

"This isn't what I'd call sunny."

"It doesn't have to burn your retinas to brighten a room." She set her roller in its tray. "This is the perfect shade. Like a few drops of juice from a lemon were squeezed into a can of white paint."

Nate rolled his eyes. "Two words—*resale value*."

"Where'd you come up with that?" Sara handed a bottle of water to Nate before unscrewing the cap on another for herself.

"I told you," Nate said, carefully cutting a line of paint around the windowsill. "I've watched a lot of DIY and house-flipping shows."

"First of all, I'm just moving in. I shouldn't have to be considering resale value." She rolled her eyes, even though he wasn't looking at her. "And second, this house will never be sold. It's the judge's mansion, remember? The next judge can paint the walls whatever color they like."

After a few minutes of silence, with each of them facing opposite walls as they painted, Nate said, "You really were impressive in court this week. Would never have known it was your first time on the bench."

Was Nate extending an olive branch?

"Thank you," Sara replied without turning around. More silence before she continued. "You've been doing an excellent job at keeping me safe. I can see why your company is so successful."

"It's been easy since you started cooperating more." An awkward pause, as if he realized how that sounded. "But thanks."

"At least there haven't been any texts lately." Sara wasn't sure if that was a good or bad thing. She didn't miss receiving them, but oddly, the more time that passed with no stalker incidents, the twitchier she became.

She held her breath whenever her phone beeped. She peeked outside from between parted curtains before stepping through the front door. And it infuriated her. She resented having her life disrupted by a veritable embodiment of evil.

After inhaling and exhaling a few deep breaths, Sara brought her thoughts back from the dark side. Having no control over the stalker situation, she needed to focus on things she *could* control. And one of those happened to be the house. She found the idea of living here for a few months without making it at least somewhat her own unacceptable.

When they were finished painting the kitchen, Sara asked, "Want a sandwich for lunch?"

"Sure." Nate put everything with paint on it into a bucket. "I'll take these outside and hose them off."

Sara juggled an armload of sandwich makings to the dining room table from a cooler she'd loaded earlier. With most of the kitchen covered with plastic tarps, she'd planned ahead. By the time Nate came back in, two plates of food rested on new placemats and Sara sat patiently in front of one. She'd set two bottles of iced tea on coasters.

"Wow. This looks great." He slid into the chair across from her and picked up half of his sandwich in one smooth move. "You know, I think you were right about that yellow after all. It does make the room more cheerful."

Sara opened the bag of chips and shook some onto her plate. "Exactly. The white felt drab."

"And the best thing about it—" he shoved a chip in his mouth "—it coordinates so well with the green stove."

She chuckled. "You jest, but maybe that's why I chose yellow."

After a few minutes of silence while they ate, Nate said, "Mind if I ask you something?"

The bite of sandwich sliding down Sara's throat landed in her stomach like a rock. In her experience, any question that needed permission to be asked usually led to an uncomfortable conversation. "Ask away."

"Why is becoming a district judge so important to you?"

Sara toyed with a chip on her plate. Her career choice certainly had nothing to do with her parents. Their only influence had been setting an example of what *not* to do with her life, and she avoided discussing them whenever possible. It might've been water under the bridge, but it was filthy water.

"I guess for me, it started when I was a kid. Some of my happiest moments were during the summers I spent with my grandfather. Back then he was a district judge in Hudson County, northwest of Austin, and he often let me go to court with him when I was staying there." She looked up to find Nate watching her as if hanging on her every word. "I loved everything about it. The stately old building, the reverential silence in the courtroom—even the desk in his chambers, always neat and orderly."

Nate nodded as if he understood. "So you wanted to make him proud by following in his footsteps?"

He doesn't get it after all. And she wanted him to understand it, to understand her. "I'm not going to lie and say his pride in me means nothing. But that wasn't why I wanted to become a judge." She sipped tea, searching for the right words. "Pops has always been a virtuous man, with a strong moral compass. He was a fair and honest judge, strict but also compassionate, making sure justice was served but not abused. *That's* what motivated me to become a judge. I don't want to just squander my life away, accomplishing nothing of value. I want to make a difference in the world, like he has."

"He sounds like one hell of a man." Nate's sincere tone warmed Sara. "I'd like to meet him someday."

"He is." Sara smiled. "And you might if I can convince him to come visit me while I'm here. And, um, if you happen to be in town at the same time."

Nate popped another chip into his mouth. "The day you arrived, you mentioned that taking this *county* judge position was a means to an end. You really compare living in Resolute to paying your dues?"

Sara puffed out her cheeks, annoyed with herself. She

hadn't meant to belittle Nate's hometown. "I didn't mean it that way. There's nothing wrong with being a county judge in a small town. I guess I'm looking at this as a stepping stone on the way to the goal I've had since I was twelve."

"Then this doesn't *have* to be a stepping stone. I get that there are different types of courts, but you've already attained your dream of becoming a judge. And a respected one in record time, no less. Seems like everywhere we've been around town, folks like you. You've got friends." His lips kicked up at the corners. "You even have your very own lemonade-painted house. Who in their right mind would leave all of that?"

"Big talk from a man about to move to California." Sara kept her tone light, but she watched Nate closely. Since he'd be heading back to the Golden State soon, why did he care if she stayed in Resolute or not?

After pushing his plate back, he tapped a beat on the table edge with his thumbs. "Well, technically I already moved there. I'm just returning."

"Why there? What's the SoCal pull that you can't resist—the weather, the wealth or the women?"

A full-bodied laugh broke out of Nate. "I just happened to be on the West Coast when I started my company." He stood and stacked the dirty plates together, effectively ending *that* portion of their conversation without answering her second question.

What a hypocrite. Clearly it was fine for the big, bad bodyguard to poke into her personal business, but when it came to revealing anything about himself, all he gave her was a cold shoulder.

Fine. Who cares what the attraction to California is about?

Apparently she did. When she couldn't shut out the images of gorgeous, tanned women with big assets in tiny bikinis lounging by pools, she changed the topic. "I'm thinking after lunch, we should move the *definitely don't want downstairs* curiosities and whatnot into the attic before we start painting the breakfast room." She watched for his reaction. For someone used to paying professionals for physical labor, she wasn't sure how far she could push Nate before he decided enough was enough.

"Give me five minutes to check the score for the game, then I'm all yours." He disappeared upstairs.

True to his word, he met her in front of a door at the opposite end of the hall from the master. It opened to reveal the attic stairs, and she led the way up to a space that stretched across the entire house. They easily stood upright, only needing to duck down where the slanted roof met the walls.

"Hmm. Looks like most of the *curiosities* are already up here." Sara picked up a bowl fashioned from a box-turtle shell.

Nate pointed at a bunch of old dolls sitting on a table, eyes open. "Those are downright creepy."

"Think those are creepy? You should see this." She waved him over to an antique cradle. Moth-eaten blankets filled the spaces around a doll. "I took a Victorian-history class in college. That's a grave doll."

Nate stared inside the cradle. "As in comparison to a happy doll?"

"It's a wax effigy." Talking about it made her mouth suddenly dry. "An exact likeness of a child who died. Possibly the son of the man who built this house."

"Maybe this stuff should be given to a museum or something." He met Sara's gaze. "I sure as hell wouldn't want to live here knowing this was right over my head."

"I'll check into that. Maybe Cassie knows." Sara moved a faded seamstress form against a wall. "Don't you think it's strange none of the other families who've lived here since got rid of this stuff?"

Nate shrugged. "Maybe it's all cursed and if you remove it from the house it reappears, ready to take revenge on you." He let out an evil laugh and grabbed Sara from behind.

Surprised, she let out a small shriek and swung her arms up and back. The knuckles of her left hand made contact with his face, and Nate grunted. Sara spun around to find him holding a hand over his eye.

"Don't worry." He lowered his hand, tears flowing from the eye. "I'm fine."

"I wasn't worried. And it serves you right. You almost scared the bejesus out of me." Sara peered closer at his eye, the white part completely bloodshot. "But you should probably go rinse it out, make sure there's no dirt in it." She rubbed her hands along the sides of her thighs, realizing how dusty they were.

"I'm really—"

"Please. Rinse it, then go watch the rest of the hockey game. I can move stuff up here by myself."

"Well, if you're sure. It *is* burning a little."

"I am. Go." Sara urged him toward the stairs.

He turned, and she noticed the very corner of his mouth twitch. She'd been had. But she wouldn't get mad, she'd get even. The court was closed all week for Thanksgiving, and Nate Reed was about to spend the next four very long days with a honey-do list.

Chapter Eight

Sara and Nate pulled up to the ranch just before noon on Thanksgiving Day. She leaned to look past him from the passenger side of his truck. "Interesting," she said. "They leave the door open so anybody strolling past can come in, or am I special?"

Nate shrugged. "Between the nice day and everything that's cooking in the kitchen, Adam most likely opened the doors for ventilation." He must have caught the flat expression on her face because he added, "And yes, you are definitely special."

She'd been half joking, half fishing for a compliment, so his answer warmed her. When they stepped from the truck, delectable aromas washed over them.

Nate inhaled. "Mmm-mmm. Glad we skipped breakfast and left plenty of room for all the good stuff."

Sara carried the holiday flower arrangement she'd insisted on buying since she hadn't been permitted to bring a side dish. It had been her solution to not showing up empty-handed. Her stomach grumbled. "You're not kidding, but what on earth is that racket? Sounds like a herd of baby elephants inside."

Nate chuckled. "Welcome to your first Reed holiday

meal. Not sure if you'll survive to tell stories about it, but it's guaranteed not to be boring."

"I don't doubt that for a minute."

A moment before they stepped into the doorway, Noah announced their arrival. "Sara and Nate are finally here."

"How does he do that?" Sara asked Nate.

"Even though we're not identical, we have that twin sixth sense."

Cassie came up to her and threw a welcoming hug around her shoulders. "What a beautiful arrangement."

Sara handed over the floral centerpiece, giving her friend a wry grin. "My contribution since you wouldn't let me bring anything else."

"There's just so much food already. Seemed pointless to add more. But thank you. Give me a sec to make room for this on the table."

After Cassie dashed off, Sara followed Nate's lead and hung her jacket on the overloaded coat rack near the front door. The place was packed. Bishop and Bree were fighting over the TV remote, arguing about which teams would win today's football games. Rachel and an older woman stood at the base of the stairs.

"Sara." Rachel waved her over. "This is my mom, Martina."

"I've heard a lot of good things about you." Martina, holding the sound-asleep Daisy in her arms, smiled at Sara.

"Thank you." A blush warmed her cheeks. She gazed at the slumbering one-year-old, a rush of some unfamiliar feeling she couldn't even name running through her. "I don't know how anyone can sleep through all this racket."

"Thank God for small favors," Rachel whispered.

Daisy's older brother, Brad, played on the floor with toy

cars. Occasionally he'd leap to his feet, pound upstairs, then return with another one.

Noah was fetching drinks for everyone, and she assumed Adam was in the kitchen. That meant with the addition of her and Nate, there were eleven people. Bigger by far than any family holiday she'd ever been to.

"Have a seat." Noah handed her a glass of white wine. "Nate mentioned you like the Hill Country Riesling, so there's plenty chilling in the fridge."

"Indeed I do." She took a sip. "Thank you." Finally, something to smooth the edges of her social anxiety. Although everyone here was so friendly that most of her uneasiness had already disappeared.

Sara chose to sit in the oversized leather recliner, while Nate squeezed his rather large frame onto the couch between Noah and Bishop, a groan escaping him.

"You sound like you used to in the morning after a high school football game." Noah handed him a beer.

"Pretty much sums up how I feel." He squirmed on the couch as he tried to find a more comfortable position.

Sara favored him with an evil grin, knowing she was the cause of his aches and pains.

He turned a hard eye on her. "I've spent the past five days painting walls, hauling stuff up to the attic and rearranging furniture."

Sara widened her eyes in feigned innocence. "All this complaining about a few tiny chores. If I'd known what a baby you'd be about it…"

"Well, he is the baby of the family." Noah chuckled, earning him a glare from his younger-by-three-minutes twin.

Bishop uncrossed his legs to avoid resting his shoe on Nate's knee, laughing as he did. "Guess I shouldn't ask how the bodyguarding is going."

"No, you shouldn't. It's not going much better than it was when Sara got here. There haven't been any texts or incidents for the past week, which is putting us even more on edge." Nate rested his head against the back of the couch and closed his eyes, giving Sara a moment to notice the worry lines and creases on his face, deeper than just a week ago. For the first time, she appreciated that her troubles were his troubles. "We're hunting one very persistent, very invisible stalker."

Bishop sipped from a glass of iced herbal tea. "That's what Cassie was telling me. She usually leaves her job at the office, but this one's got her frustrated. She mentioned she wants to talk to you both later. Something about reviewing prison records."

So, her troubles were Nate's troubles. And they were Cassie's, too. And Adam's and Noah's. And that meant to a lesser degree, their significant others as well. And all this time Sara had thought she was in this mess by herself.

Having an entire family behind her was something new, and she found the notion both pleasing and embarrassing. It wasn't like she was related by blood or was even a significant other. And she'd always fought her own battles. And yet…

"Good. Hopefully she and Adam have uncovered something we can work with." Nate scooped a few pecans from the bowl Noah was holding and popped them into his mouth. Then, completely changing the subject, he asked Bishop, "Any luck tracking down our mom?"

Cassie walked back into the room and placed the flowers on a beautiful hand-hewn fireplace mantel. "Sorry, Sara. We can move these to the table after we eat, but there's going to be way too much food on it during dinner."

"That's fine. I didn't even think about that." Centerpieces had worked on her childhood dining table because the dishes and people had been fewer. She'd gladly trade elegant flower arrangements for loving people any day of the week.

Bishop nodded in response to Nate. "I've got a possible lead, but I'll have to travel to check it out." He smiled apologetically at his wife. "But Cassie prefers I don't leave until after the long weekend."

"Probably for the best. Traffic's always crazy on holidays. Keep me posted." Nate stood. "Noah, want a beer?"

"Bro. It's not about want, it's about need. And I do need one. Gotta have one with football, and today is all about football." Using the remote, he changed the channel from one game to another amid a chorus of protests. "Hey, chill out. Just checking on the score. I'll flip it back."

Bishop scoffed. "I think today is about more than just football."

"Oh, you mean the parade?" Noah's straight face dissolved into laughter.

"I'll bring you a beer." Nate left them to debate the meaning of Thanksgiving and headed toward the kitchen.

Not entirely sure why, Sara got up and followed him. Maybe it was the strange, unreadable look on his face as he walked from the room. He seemed preoccupied with something, and she didn't want her stalker problems to ruin the day for him.

She moved through the kitchen with simmering pots on the stove, pausing to breathe in the mouth-watering aromas before continuing through the open door to the back patio. Nate was pulling an iced-down bottle of beer from a galvanized tub near the back door, so she strolled past him and took in the backyard activity.

Rachel played catch with five-year-old Brad while Martina stood in the shade, holding the now wide-awake Daisy on her hip. Adam sat in a patio chair, gazing at the idyllic scene with a smile on his lips. Sara vaguely remembered Adam from her first visit. Seemed that Mr. Serious, as she'd dubbed him then, had wound up with his high school crush and her two adorable kids.

Sara had never given any thought to having children. No reason to when she'd never been in a relationship long enough for it to be a consideration. Besides, she had no idea how to be a good mother, and she sure as hell wouldn't risk subjecting her own kids to a childhood like hers had been. She might not've been consumed with international partying, like her parents, but her focus was centered solely on her career. The idea of having children had always been a distant, hazy concept—one better considered in that mythical place called Someday Land.

Martina set the toddler down, and as the little girl grasped her grandmother's finger and tugged her toward Brad, an unfamiliar twang of maternal longing hit Sara square in the chest. Chalking it up to Daisy waddle-walking in her cute fall outfit, she quickly shook off the feeling and poured herself another glass of wine from the bottle some brilliant person here had set in the icy beer tub.

"Hey, Nate," Adam said. "Why don't you grab a chair for Sara and the two of you sit with me a spell?"

While Nate stepped away to comply with his older brother's request, Sara took the moment alone with Adam to say, "Nice family you have."

"Crazy, isn't it? One day I'm single, and the next I'm almost married with kids. But I'm one lucky son of a gun. Martina is the perfect future mother-in-law, Brad and Daisy are great and Rachel…well, she's my world."

What would it be like to be someone's world?

Nate joined them, carrying two chairs. Once they were settled, Adam took a pull on his beer and the three of them chatted a while, his eyes never leaving Rachel and the kids. Then he asked Nate, "Anything new on the stalker?"

Nate cringed. The gesture was barely noticeable, but she marked it. "Not a damn thing, but my gut's telling me the bastard hasn't left the area."

"That's what Cassie and I think, too. We have some possible candidates to go over with you two, but to be honest, we're not convinced any of them is our guy."

Sara's hope deflated, but like Nate, she worked on not letting it show. "We could at least eliminate some of them, couldn't we?"

"That's the plan." Adam stood.

"Maybe after dinner?" Nate suggested.

"Or between football games. We'll play it by ear." Adam lifted the grill's lid, revealing an assortment of vegetables. "I thought I'd get off easy this year, roasting the turkey and everyone else bringing side dishes. But nooo, I have to make Bishop his special grilled veggies to go with his turkey."

"If this family didn't put sausage in the dressing and bacon in the beans, I wouldn't need anything special." Bishop leaned over the grill and inhaled. "But I'm kinda glad you do because your grilling skills are amazing, Adam. So very, very amazing, just like you." He wrapped an arm around Adam's neck and planted a loud kiss on his brother-in-law's cheek.

"Whoa." Noah joined the group, laughing. "You're barely back from your honeymoon, Bishop. And already cheating on my sister?"

Cassie leaned out through the kitchen door. "Honey, please stop flirting with my brother before we all wind up on a reality show."

"Sorry, Cassie. But you know I can't help myself." Bishop failed miserably at keeping a straight face. "Adam's grilled veggies are just so special."

Everyone on the patio cracked up as Noah dropped onto the chair Adam had just vacated, a longneck bottle in one hand. "Bro, I thought you were bringing me a beer. Guess if I want something done around here, I have to do it myself."

Nate scanned the yard. "Where's Bree? I haven't seen her since we got here."

"Her sweet potatoes weren't quite ready, and she figured since the ovens here were already being used, she'd finish them at the casita."

"So, how's it going with you two?" Nate asked his twin. "Y'all like living in Adam's old cabin?"

"Are you kidding? That place is *sa-weet*. We told Rachel she's welcome to come watch the sunsets anytime she wants." Noah gave him a lopsided grin. "Long as she doesn't bring Adam along. He might decide he made a mistake and never leave."

Noah explained to Sara that years ago their older brother had moved into the largest of several cabins on the Reed property and spent a considerable amount of time and money renovating the place. Unfortunately, though large, it only had one bedroom and Rachel had two kids. So despite his affection for the place, Adam had moved back into the main house with his new family. And Noah and Bree had been the recipients of a cabin worthy of a cable-network renovation show.

Everyone laughed at Noah's story except Nate, and Sara wondered why.

Fifteen minutes later, Bree returned with her famous praline sweet potatoes and the meal began. Everyone moved back inside to the dining room and took their seats. Rounding the table with a heavy platter of carved turkey, Adam held it for each person while they served themselves.

Sara held a spoonful of sweet potatoes over her plate, searching for an empty spot. With her past holidays shared with only one or two people, she'd never attended a true family Thanksgiving dinner before. Apparently her eyes were three times the size of her stomach. She would've felt ashamed of the mountain of food in front of her, except everyone else's plates were piled higher than hers.

"White meat okay?" Adam set the platter on the table next to her. When Sara nodded, he covered her side dishes with slices of turkey. "Next year, remember to leave room for the main dish. Though I will admit, everything tastes pretty good all mashed together."

She couldn't believe she'd forgotten about the turkey. "I can see why you didn't want Nate and me to bring more food," she said to Cassie. "I'm surprised the table can support all of this as it is."

"Believe it or not, Adam used to make everything himself." Cassie scooped Rachel's cheesy green beans with bacon onto her plate. "I never thought he'd relinquish control like this."

Adam snorted. "If the twins were cooking, I wouldn't have. And we all know the only thing you can make is a trip to the diner for one of Marge's homemade pies."

Cassie shrugged. "Hey, I play to my strengths and acknowledge my weaknesses. I'm not now and never have been a cook."

"We can all attest to that." Noah looked at Sara. "If Adam hadn't taught himself to cook at the tender age of ten, we'd all have perished from malnutrition before puberty."

Laughing, Sara passed along the sweet potatoes and took a long drink of cold white wine. Between the heat outside and all the bodies inside, Adam had finally turned on the air-conditioning, but it was still fighting to lower the dining room's temperature.

As the meal continued, she realized the anxiety that had bothered her when she'd first walked into the house had dissipated. Typically, she avoided large gatherings because she abhorred small talk and, worse, sitting alone while everyone else talked and laughed and had fun. That same fear had grabbed her today, but between family anecdotes and good-natured teasing, she'd forgotten about being nervous.

Across the table, Nate's brown eyes twinkled as he raised his glass toward her in a silent toast. She lifted hers too, her lips curving upward. The heat that filled her had nothing to do with the stuffy room or the wine. It was the warmth of family. Of friends. Of Nate.

"…wouldn't share his toy, even then." Martina finished a story about Brad, and everyone laughed. Sara pretended to. She'd been lost in Nate's eyes instead of paying attention.

"You've got to pick up the pace, Sara." Noah poked his fork in the air toward her plate. "You snooze, you lose around this table."

"I'm about to be snoozing—between all this food and wine." She wiped her mouth with her napkin. "If you don't have doggy bags, I'll just take a piece of foil over my plate."

Cassie laughed. "Trust me, there's more than enough to send some home with everyone."

"Ladies, y'all outdid yourselves with your most excellent side dishes." Adam raised his glass. "I hereby declare all future holidays will forever be potluck."

"To potluck." Everyone toasted.

"And here's to Adam." Bishop held his iced tea aloft. "For all the meals he's cooked by himself, as well as his meat-free variations."

Everyone chanted, "To Adam."

Sara raised her glass along with everyone else, but her mind wasn't in the room. The holidays since becoming an adult that she hadn't been able to spend with her grandfather, those days she'd thought she enjoyed alone in her apartment, lounging in sweats and binge-watching TV while eating delivery from upscale restaurants paled in comparison to this gathering. But how could she have known? Without this experience, she might never have discovered, even if for just one day, what it was like to be part of a loving family.

But now that she had, she was afraid she'd never be content without one.

STANDING AND TAKING a well-deserved bow, Adam checked his watch. "Are you ready for some football?" he shouted.

"Football!" came the enthusiastic reply, and the crowd rose from the table and moved toward the living room.

Nate looked back when he noticed Sara wasn't next to him. She still sat at the table, a perplexed expression on her face.

"Um, shouldn't we put away the food first?" she asked.

"Ha! What a rookie you are, Sara." Reaching past her, Noah shoved a piece of turkey into a roll, dipped it in gravy and held a napkin beneath it. "Trust me, by the time half-time rolls around, everyone will have made at least one trip to the table for leftovers. Tell her, bro."

"He's right." Nate held up an empty wine bottle. "Want a refill?"

"I'm not sure if I should. I don't usually have more than one glass."

"It's a four-day weekend. Live a little."

She deliberated for a moment. "Why not?"

They went into the kitchen, and Nate grabbed another chilled bottle, popped the cork and refilled her glass. Then he headed outside to grab himself another beer, pleased when she stayed with him instead of joining his family in the living room.

"Listen, I'm stuffed to the gills." He patted his belly. "Do you feel like taking a walk? Help settle some of this food?"

Sara nodded. "That would be great. If I sit down now, I'm afraid I'll be asleep in an instant."

"We can't have that. It would be embarrassing for you if everyone heard how loudly you snore."

"What? I do *not* snore."

"Really? Then the noise I hear coming from your room at night must be a grizzly bear driving a bulldozer." Nate fought a smile. "I'm going to have to climb up on the roof and tack down the shingles you've blown loose."

"Hardy har har. And here I thought Noah was supposed to be the funny one." She laughed.

He gave her a sheepish grin. "I have my moments."

"Not enough of them." She ducked her head, her smile lingering.

"Touché."

He liked her this way, with her hair down, having fun. "Come on," he invited with a head nod. "Let me show you around the place."

The day had cooled now that the sun was dropping, but it was still warm enough that neither needed a jacket. He set a leisurely pace as he led her around to the front, down the driveway and out across the land that surrounded the main house.

Sara turned in a circle, taking it all in. "There are so many trees on your land."

"Mostly live oaks and mesquite. And then we've got

all those fruit and pecan trees behind the house." About to
tell her about the creek running through their property, he
snapped his mouth shut. Sara already knew about the creek.
About how good its cool water felt on a warm day. About
the grasses and wildflowers along its banks, tall enough
in the spring to conceal two young lovers.

She studied his face. "Why don't you like talking about
this?"

He worried she'd read his mind and pretended to be confused. "About the ranch?" Nate prided himself on his ability to be reserved, to project an impression of aloofness. A
necessary survival skill learned while growing up at odds
with his father's wishes. So what was it Sara thought she
saw when she looked at him?

"Not just the ranch." When he didn't reply, she added,
"It's your face that gives you away, you know."

"Remind me not to play poker with you." He chuckled.
"So, what exactly is my face telling you?" He continued
to smile, although the direction of this conversation made
him feel like a long-tailed cat in a rocking chair factory. To
gird himself, he lifted his beer and took a drink.

"When Noah was explaining about why Adam moved
back into the main house, your face shut down. When he
talked about moving into Adam's cabin with Bree, you
grew distant." She arched a brow. "When you were watching Rachel play with the kids, your eyes glazed over and
you disappeared completely."

Stunned, Nate tried to gather his thoughts. How had
Sara homed in on his...what? Wistful regret? Bittersweet
longing for something he'd deemed unnecessary? No one
else had ever noticed, let alone thought to ask him about it.

He paused then, not sure how much to explain. Did he
even want to wade into the muck of his feelings on the mat-

ter? He glanced at Sara and found her watching him, like she really wanted to hear what he had to say. It could have been the wine that made her glistening eyes appear interested, but he preferred to think it was because she cared. And seeing that concern, his inhibition slipped away.

"I've always felt like the odd man out in my family. The one who didn't want to be a deputy. The one who couldn't join in on dinner conversations because they revolved around law enforcement. The one who came home from California for holidays, only to envy my siblings' tight bond with our father and each other, their private jokes and common interests."

He shrugged as if trying to convince himself he was immune to the hurt. "I created a barrier between myself and the others through the decisions *I* made."

And today that realization had become a huge clear bubble surrounding his amazing extended family, leaving him on the outside looking in. His siblings had all found their perfect matches, with Adam bringing kids and a future mother-in-law along for the ride. Even Sara had looked like she belonged here more than Nate.

"It's never too late to change things, if you really want to." Sara's compassionate smile almost did him in. "Come on, let's take that walk."

They strolled together in companionable silence, each alone with their own thoughts. When Sara stepped on uneven ground and lost her balance, Nate grabbed her arm to steady her.

"Lord, I'm such a klutz."

She looked up into his eyes, that signature blush of hers covering her cheeks. Convincing himself that he didn't care about her anymore was a losing battle. He lowered his head slowly, giving her time to say no or push him away. But she didn't. Her soft lips met his in a long, tender kiss, an almost perfect reenactment of their first one so many years ago.

He finally pulled back. "We better head back to the house before we're labeled antisocial."

"Or worse, anti-football." She coughed out a small, nervous laugh and dropped her gaze.

But Nate took her hand as they headed back to the house, and this time the silence between them swelled with unspoken emotions.

WHEN THE BREAK came between games, a synchronized flurry of activity took place. The table was cleared, leftovers packed into the fridge and dishes rinsed. Nate couldn't help but chuckle to himself. While it was usually the twins' job to do the dishes, Noah would get stuck with it all tonight.

With only minutes left until the next kickoff, Adam huddled with Sara and Nate. "Cassie and I want to meet with you at the sheriff's office tomorrow to go over the list of possible criminal suspects. It's just too crazy here today."

"Clearer heads. I agree." Sara nodded.

Nate scrutinized her expression, wondering if she was referring to the alcoholic beverages or their kiss.

"We've got pie," Cassie called. "And coffee."

Everyone gathered around the dining room table, which held four varieties of the sweet dessert.

"What's your poison?" Noah asked Sara as he handed her a small plate.

"All that refined sugar is exactly that—poison," Bishop said, and the entire group groaned.

Noah rolled his eyes. "Cassie, make that health nut shut up."

"Believe me, I've tried."

"With so many to choose from, I'm having a hard time deciding." Sara rounded the table. "Y'all must really love pie."

The others looked at each other and broke out laughing.

"What's so funny?" Sara looked around, confused.

"You kinda had to be there," Noah said.

"Noah's obsession with pie almost killed Adam and Rachel's chance for their happily-ever-after." Nate pulled her closer and whispered, "I'll tell you the details later."

"Now that you've piqued my curiosity, you better." She slid a small piece of pecan pie onto her plate.

Settled again in front of the TV with dessert and coffee, the group watched, yelled and cursed their way through the second game.

Sara sat between Nate and the couch arm, leaning into him as the food, wine and fun seemed to take its toll on her.

"How 'bout I take you home?" She tilted her head to look up at him.

"I have a better idea." He touched the end of her nose. "How 'bout *I* take *you* home?"

"That's a much better idea. I should've thought of that." Sara pushed off from Nate's thigh and the armrest to get to her feet. Addressing the room, she said, "Thank you all for the wonderful Thanksgiving."

Cassie hugged her before Nate steered her to the coat-rack and started to help her with her jacket.

"I don't think I need that." Sara pressed her hands to her cheeks. "I'm pretty warm."

"Humor me." After she was zipped into hers, Nate pulled on his jacket and opened the front door.

"Whoa. It *is* cold out here." She huddled up against him in the truck while they waited for the engine to warm up.

He didn't regret kissing her. Not one bit. But now he

needed to focus on the reason they were together. He was her bodyguard; she was his client. Period.

Nate sighed. They'd be alone in that big house tonight, the desire ignited by their kiss burning a hole straight through him.

It was going to be one long, lonely night.

Chapter Nine

On the drive home from the Thanksgiving shindig, Sara basked in a warm feeling of belonging. The raucous conversations, family anecdotes and chaotic fun had nearly overwhelmed her, as her only experiences with holidays while growing up had been awkward meals with her self-absorbed parents. And that was only when they'd been in town. Most years as a child she'd spent quiet Thanksgivings with her grandfather, and she still did. And though she loved that old man to the moon and back, Reed family shindigs were incredible.

She still felt a little guilty about not spending the holiday with him this year, but Pops had encouraged her to join her friends. Despite approaching ninety, he'd assured her he'd be around for next year's holidays.

Her mind drifted to another topic, and she murmured, "Hmm."

"Hmm, what?" Nate asked. The clean, woody scent of his cologne was working its magic on her.

"I was thinking about that story Cassie was telling about the first time she had a meal with Bishop. Those two seem like oil and water, yet somehow they make it work. I wonder what their secret is."

"Oh, I don't think they have a secret. They fell in love,

and the rest…" Sara felt rather than saw his shrug. "I guess they just compromise."

"You mean like whether to have steak or tofu for dinner?" She chuckled. "That's a pretty big compromise."

Within the intimate darkness of the truck, Nate's deep laugh rumbled. "Yeah, like that." He paused. "You're in an awfully good mood."

"Well, I won't lie, I did have a few glasses of that most excellent Riesling." And the ambrosia had melted away her normal reticence, filling her with confidence.

"A family favorite. Made right here in Texas at one of the local Hill Country wineries." He glanced at her, a streetlight illuminating his teasing grin. "And how exactly do you define *a few*?"

"Hmph. You're my bodyguard, not my father." Not that her father had ever advised her about public conduct. And he sure as hell hadn't set a good example for it, either. But Nate was right. She'd probably downed almost a whole bottle all by herself. She normally stopped after one glass and couldn't remember the last time she'd felt so relaxed. So happy. So warm.

Definitely not since those texts had started coming. But having Nate around dissipated her concern and made her feel safe. *I could get used to this.*

"Are you hot?"

Nate's question caught her off guard. "Hot? Me?" She checked the side window next to her and found it a little steamed up. "No, I'm fine. Why do you ask?"

"You're fanning yourself."

Sara dropped her hands into her lap, her face ironically burning with embarrassment. Thank goodness it was dark. "Habit," she lied. "When I drink too much."

Okay, I'm most definitely feeling warm, but it has little

to do with the wine. Not with Nate sitting so close. Close enough that she could reach out her hand and touch his rock-solid bicep or jean-encased thigh. For days now she'd tried to stop her inquisitive mind from imagining what it would be like to touch him. Not an accidental brush against him or his arm around her shoulder after a traumatic incident. But to really *touch* him. She sucked in a breath.

"Funny, I've never noticed you fanning yourself before."

"Well, I do."

"Good to know."

The mirth in his tone would have normally bothered her. But even if he was teasing her, he wasn't laughing *at* her.

As Nate turned down the street that led to the judge's mansion, Sara leaned her head back and tried to cool her jets. Not all the way; just enough that she wouldn't flame out. While her libido calmed, her mind wandered again to the time when she and Nate had hooked up before. Had she felt the same overwhelming need for him back then?

The attraction had been there, still…in her mind something seemed different, something elusive about her current emotions.

"You enjoy yourself today?"

Did he even need to ask? "Yes. It was a first for me."

Her comment clearly confused him. "First what?"

How could someone like him understand what her world had been like? "First large family gathering on a holiday. Usually, Thanksgiving and Christmas were just my grandfather and me. The last time I experienced this much commotion and fun was the last time I was here. I absolutely loved it."

"I thought maybe we were too much for you."

"Not at all. I was a bit apprehensive at first. I had the mistaken impression—probably from too many TV shows—

that family get-togethers were rife with feuds and gossip. But your family is just how I remember them. With a few new faces, of course." She kicked herself mentally for bringing up the time she'd walked away from him.

Ever the gentleman, he ignored it. "I'm glad."

His words were soft, and she realized in that moment just how important her answer was to him. *I may be wine-happy, but I'm beginning to understand why what I'm feeling now is different.*

With the younger version of Nate, she'd been content with a fling. But with the adult Nate, she wanted… Well, she wanted more.

Ironic, how easily she'd once dismissed Nate's own desire for more. Although of legal age, he'd been a teenager, and teenagers seldom knew what they wanted. Still, she must have hurt him far more than she'd imagined.

His life these days was rooted in California, which meant *more* wasn't in the cards, but there was no reason why she couldn't have the here and now, was there?

Heat flowed through her body, a heady mixture of desire, need and determination. She'd seen Nate observing her when he'd thought she wasn't watching. Those smoldering looks aroused her in ways she couldn't describe. And he wouldn't have eyed her that way if the feelings weren't mutual. For all that he pretended otherwise, he wasn't made of stone.

They reached the driveway and parked, and that fast the carefree Nate she'd seen earlier in the evening disappeared and protector Nate emerged. "Stay here, doors locked, until I clear the garage."

"Aye, aye, captain." She knew the routine and hated the need for it. Hated how this damn stalker was affecting her very existence. Redecorating the house had provided her with a brief sense of empowerment, but the work was nearly finished. She needed to find another way to feel in control of at least one aspect of her life.

She inhaled the lingering scent of Nate's cologne, and the solution was obvious.

NATE MADE A QUICK, thorough search of the garage before dashing back to the truck. He didn't like leaving Sara out in the open, locked vehicle or not, but this was the safest way. Parking inside, he locked the garage and led her inside the house, his head on a swivel.

With the front door locked, he took hold of her shoulders. "Stay here while I clear the house."

No *aye, aye* this time, but she did give him a compliant salute. Nate swallowed against the lump in his throat. Tipsy Sara was as alluring as hell.

He returned from his sweep to find her exactly where he'd left her, leaning against the doorframe, eyes closed, humming to herself.

Dang if she didn't make it hard to stay professional.

She seemed unaware when he stood inches away from her. So close, he could watch her heartbeats pulse in the hollow of her throat, identify the subtle hint of citrus and spice on her skin, see the smattering of pale freckles across the arch of her nose.

He reached his hand forward, brushing her cheek in a feather-like touch just as her eyes drifted open and gazed directly into his.

"I like your cologne," she whispered, a lazy smile curling her lips.

"Um, thanks." He keyed in the code on the alarm panel just over her left shoulder.

"Oh." Her smile faltered. "You're just setting the alarm."

"I am." His tone was as soft as hers. He locked eyes with her, gauging her reaction to his nearness. The signals she'd been giving him all night were undeniable. He wanted to respond, to give them both what they wanted.

But this wasn't how he conducted business. This wasn't how he treated Cassie's friends. Hell, this wasn't how he treated women in general. He backed away. "I'm going to check the monitors."

"Why, if the house is clear?"

"To see if there was any activity while we were gone."

"Oh."

Was that disappointment he heard in her voice? Practically speed walking to the breakfast room where he'd set up the monitors, he spent way longer than necessary reviewing camera footage for the stalker. No sign of the bastard. At least one thing was right tonight.

After enough time had passed that he thought she'd be asleep, he heard soft footsteps behind him.

"Nate?"

He turned around and stopped breathing. Her face was scrubbed clean, her feet bare. Like some dewy-eyed innocent, Sara stood framed in the doorway, her white silk robe backlit by a kitchen light. If she wore anything underneath it, he saw no evidence. What he could see, quite clearly, were the outlines of her pert nipples. "I thought you were going to bed."

"That's my plan." She bit her bottom lip, and Nate shifted in his chair.

"What's stopping you?"

"You are."

"Me? I'm not stopping you. If you want to go to bed, go. I'll turn off the lights in here."

Sara sighed. "I must not be very good at this."

"Good at what?" Nate felt like a jerk trying to play dumb. Her signals hadn't been mixed tonight, and he knew what Sara was leading up to.

Her head tilted to one side as if in deliberation. Then she straightened. "I want to go to bed *with you*."

And there she was, the confident woman Sara had been at twenty-one, taking charge of their first night together.

Nate stood, searching for a way to stop something that would not end well for either of them. "Look, this kind of thing happens all the time. Perfectly normal. A client often comes to feel affection for the person protecting them. Trust me, the feelings will pass. Best to ignore them."

Sara glided farther into the room. "Nate?"

He stood rooted, completely transfixed by the image of her swaying hips and flowing robe. He forced out a gravelly reply. "What?"

She floated up to him and placed the flat of her hands on his chest. "I don't want to ignore the feelings. And I don't think this has anything to do with protector infatuation."

She gazed up at him, her wide, trusting eyes hopeful with anticipation. Her lips parted as she drew breath. "Kiss me, Nate."

And he was undone.

He slid a hand behind her neck, cupping her head and pulling her closer until their lips almost touched. "You have no idea what you're doing to me."

"Oh, I think I do."

Her arms wrapped around his waist until her body was flush with his, her soft curving warmth the perfect counter to his hardness.

"Sara, you're making it impossible for me to—"

"Am I?" She rose on her tiptoes and brushed her lips lightly against his. "I want this, Nate. I want you."

Their lips remained touching, and he breathed her in. "There's no future in this." His words were muffled against her.

"I know."

"I'm leaving soon for California."

"I know."

"Sara…" He took possession of her mouth.

She parted her lips, and the sweetness of her tongue, thrashing with his, had him pulling her even more tightly against him.

Her hands slid under his shirt and ran the length of his back, then slipped lower. He let her have her way, not daring to break their kiss, not daring to touch her in return for fear she would realize her mistake.

And then she pulled away.

Nate's groan reflected the agony of the break, both mentally and physically.

Breathless herself, Sara's chest rose and fell as she reached out and took his hand. Without a word, he followed her as she led him upstairs to her bedroom.

Soft music played, several candles were lit and the bed covers had been turned down. This seduction of hers was not the result of too much wine. It was careful and deliberate. And if inspired by their days of close proximity, he no longer cared.

She let go of his hand, turned to face him and dropped her robe.

Seeing a naked woman was nothing new to Nate. But Sara standing nude before him with her shoulders back and head held high…this was something altogether different. Her assertive stance, in stark contrast to her bare-skinned vulnerability, called to him on a primal level.

He wanted her, wanted to devour her until she was a part

of him. At the same time, he was consumed by an over-whelming need to be gentle, to explore the exquisite contours of her body with unhurried care and skill.

He chose the latter.

As Sara reached for his belt and unbuckled it, Nate pulled his shirt over his head and tossed it to the floor. His shoes and the rest of his clothes soon joined it, and he scooped her up into his arms.

He laid her back on the bed and stretched out beside her, propping himself on one elbow while his other hand traced the contours of her face, her neck, her shoulders. Continuing downward with his caresses, he palmed her breasts and gently teased her nipples before tracing a line down her flat belly. Though she parted her legs for him, ready for his touch, he continued down, stroking the insides of her thighs before trailing back up to her navel.

Sara's hand grabbed hold of his wrist, her eyes locked on his. "Touch me."

And without waiting for an answer, she slid his hand right where she wanted him, her eyes not closing until Nate dipped into her wetness.

He kissed the column of her throat, her collarbone, her breasts. His tongue teased her nipples while his fingers continued to caress her.

When the scent of her arousal became too much to take, his kisses moved south. And there he lost his mind to the experience. Tasting Sara, drinking her in, inhaling her essence until he groaned with need.

Sara arched against his mouth, her fingers tunneling through his hair, holding him to her. Her breaths became shorter, faster, until a low moan escaped her and she trembled from the force of her orgasm.

Nate worked his way back up her body, cherishing every

inch of skin on the way. Then her smoldering gaze pierced his heart and released a long-suppressed passion for this woman.

A satisfied smile on her face, Sara pushed Nate onto his back.

Memories surfaced of Sara as a college student, taking command of their first sexual encounter. For some reason, she'd needed to be in charge even back then.

She crawled across the bed like a leopard on the prowl and opened the nightstand drawer. She returned, and rising onto her knees, she opened the small foil packet in her hand, straddled him and rolled the condom down his hard, erect length. With a seductive smile, she leaned forward and, bracing herself with her hands on the bed, she began a slow and steady ride.

Her heat, her scent, the very feel of her soft skin sliding against his drove him mad, his decision to go slow evaporated by his burning need for her. As she continued to ride him, he laved at her nipples, grabbed hold of her bottom and matched her downward movements with hip-lifting thrusts that drove him deeper inside her.

As if not willing to relinquish control to him, Sara's inner walls tightened around him and released, tightened and released, again and again. Her nails dragged across his chest as her body stiffened, taking him with her to heights he hadn't known existed.

Sara collapsed on top of him, and they lay that way, legs intertwined, Nate's arms around her. She nestled her head against his chest with a sigh of contentment.

An unfamiliar sense of affection filled him. An emotion he'd never connected to sex before—or if he had, he'd forgotten about it. Enjoyable, but dangerous. He was leaving town in a couple of weeks, and Sara would eventually go back to Austin when this judging gig was done.

Becoming attached was not an option.

THE NEXT DAY, Sara's eyes fluttered open to find morning sunlight bathing her room in hues of gold. That and the lingering scent of lovemaking produced a broad, sated smile. She blushed, remembering her wanton behavior. Seducing Nate, then her unrestrained reactions to his maddening touch.

Their night together had reawakened feelings for Nate she'd convinced herself were long gone. She slid her hand across the bed in search of his warmth and comfort, but his side of the bed was empty.

His side of the bed. Hmm, she liked the sound of that.

Sara slipped out of bed and into the shower. As she lathered her breasts, her belly, between her thighs, the memory of Nate's hands caressing her skin sent aftershocks of pleasure through her. She was sore in the best possible way yet still brimming with need. She wanted more. More sex. More Nate.

Dressing casually, Sara headed downstairs and found Nate at the breakfast table, staring at camera footage. When she rested a hand on his shoulder, he glanced up.

"Morning, sleepyhead." He swiveled the chair, snaked his arm around her waist and hauled her into the V between his legs.

"I did sleep well." Sara ran her fingers through his hair that was still damp from a shower. "What time did you get up?"

Nate pulled her down until she was sitting on his thigh and nuzzled her cheek with his whiskers. "Not that long ago. You looked too peaceful to wake."

A sly smile appeared. "I wish you had."

"We would've spent the whole day in bed if I had, and you know it." He cupped the back of her head and gave her a deep, gentle kiss.

Standing, she said, "As much as I'm enjoying this, I really need some caffeine."

"I've got your favorite coffee loaded in the espresso machine, ready to go."

She leaned down for one more kiss, then ambled into the kitchen. Nate followed her with his empty mug, ready for a refill. When she pressed the button for coffee, the intoxicating aroma from the black elixir of life filled the air.

I wouldn't mind waking up to this treatment every morning.

"I need to finish reviewing the nighttime footage before we meet up with Cassie and Adam to go over what they've turned up on your case." Nate leaned against the counter while they waited for her mug to fill.

"Great—that'll give me time to review my upcoming court cases." Since the goose trial, she'd only dealt with a few traffic-ticket arraignments, the courtroom closed to spectators at Nate's insistence. Insistence that normally would have annoyed her, but not nearly as much as the trepidation she felt every time her text notification went off. "So, leave by nine o'clock?" She picked up her coffee and chanced scalding her tongue with the first sips.

Nate set his mug on the small platform and refilled the coffee module. "Hate to admit it, but this thing does make the best coffee in town."

She cocked her brow, her way of saying *told ya so* without words. In the back pocket of her jeans, her cell phone chirped with an incoming text. She pulled it from her pocket.

"It's probably Cassie making sure we still plan to meet," Nate said.

"It's not from Cassie." Sara tapped the screen to open the text from an unfamiliar number. Her body went rigid, the coffee she'd just swallowed churning in her stomach.

Nate tensed at her reaction. "What is it?"

"It's from *him*." Sara held up her phone so he could see her fresh horror. "According to the *Victoria Chronicle*, I'm dead."

Chapter Ten

Nate strode into the small conference room in the sheriff's department, Sara beside him. "Have we got an update for you."

Cassie and Adam, sitting next to each other at one of the tables, looked up.

"Update on what?" Adam asked.

Nate took a chair across from them as Sara slid into the one next to him.

"The latest text from my stalker." She fished her phone from her pocket and forwarded the text with the obituary to Cassie and Adam, then rested her forearms on the table, her hands shaking. He wanted to wrap an arm around her shoulders, reassure her that he'd protect her. But no public displays of affection while they worked.

Cassie read from the screen. "'Sara Diana Bennett… born in Austin…an unremarkable career with the Travis County District Attorney's Office…briefly served as a county judge during which she incurred a series of unfortunate incidents that led to her death…survived by her grandfather, Archer Bennett…no service, flowers or donations." She looked up. "This is in one of the Victoria papers?"

"Also posted on Obituaries.com for the whole world to see." The quiver in Sara's voice matched the tremble in her hands.

"It could be in other newspapers as well," Nate added. "All he had to do was mark which ones he wanted it to appear in on that one website."

"Doesn't the website have to verify the facts before they distribute it?" Adam's tone was incredulous. "At least the fact that the person is actually dead?"

"Apparently the website only cares about getting paid." Sara crossed her arms over her chest.

Cassie set her phone down. "We'll get to the bottom of this. I'll see if the website has a phone number attached to it. One way or another, we'll get ahold of someone there and find out who submitted the obituary, how they paid for it. We can backtrack from there."

"If they're located in the US, you might need to wait until Monday. Holiday staff doesn't usually include anyone who can actually deal with problems." Sara's lips formed an adult pout that, in profile, made Nate pause.

He hadn't known someone could be so angry and so cute at the same time.

"For now, let's start working on why we're here," Cassie suggested. "Getting distracted by this creep's latest antics won't help us identify him."

"I've done background searches on the names you gave me." Nate eyed his sister. "But I'm assuming you were able to access a lot more info than I could." He pulled his laptop and several file folders from his computer bag.

They were set up in the small conference room that the deputies used for morning briefings. Adam and Cassie had turned one of the tables lengthwise so they could face each other and see the front of the room without anyone turning all the way around. Cassie powered on her laptop and held out a hand for one of Nate's file folders. He passed them out, keeping one for himself.

"Once we cross-reference the criminal records we obtained with your searches, I'm hoping some possible suspects stand out." Cassie logged into the department portal.

"I'm glad you were able to request the records as part of an investigation." Sara opened her own computer to take notes. "I have a feeling if *I'd* requested a list of all my cases, the DA's office might not have obliged so quickly. Alton wasn't too happy about my quick departure." She opened the file folder Nate had handed her.

"Just so you're aware, they did want to know why we requested the list." Adam gave her a sympathetic smile.

Her brows rose. "What did you tell them?"

"That someone appeared to be harassing you and we wanted to eliminate possible threats from your court cases." Cassie shrugged when her friend's mouth dropped open. "I wasn't about to lie. And it got us the records."

"But I didn't want anyone up there to know anything about this." Sara's disappointment was palpable.

Adam frowned. "Why?"

When Sara didn't answer, Cassie piped up. "She doesn't want this to reflect on her stellar reputation in Travis County. She doesn't want her ex-boss, who stole her last case out from under her, to be glad she took off before this stalker became *his* problem to deal with." Glaring at Sara, she added, "But she doesn't seem to realize her life is more important than some smug DA's opinion of her."

His sister could be blunt. Without thinking, Nate wrapped his arm around Sara's shoulders in a comforting move. But when she smiled at him and placed her hand on top of his, he caught a knowing glance between his siblings. Nate gave her shoulder a gentle squeeze, then removed his arm.

He wasn't about to explain his and Sara's relationship to them. He was having trouble explaining it to himself.

Nate had figured his memories of what had been ten years ago, his imaginings of how things would be if they ever reconnected had been blown out of proportion over time. But if anything, his fantasies paled in comparison to last night.

He might not have gotten Sara completely out of his system yet, but there was no harm in them enjoying each other's company in order to do so, at least until he left for California. Both he and Sara could take this time to distract each other from the unpleasant reality of her stalker and get closure on what had happened between them years ago. A win-win in his book.

Cassie shared her laptop to the huge monitor attached to the front wall, opened the folder Nate had given her and flipped through printouts of his searches, sliding the criminals into the same order as she had them arranged on her computer. Closing the folder and laying a few pages on top of it, she announced, "Arthur Jenkins."

Adam, Nate and Sara extracted the same pages from their folders while Cassie read from the screen. "…charged with aggravated assault, attempted rape, resisting arrest. As he was being led from the courtroom after being sentenced to twenty years—"

"He bellowed that he was going to kill me." Sara's tone was flat, her eyes blank. "It was the first time someone threatened my life." She blinked, then refocused on their small group, a tight smile stretching her lips. "But it wasn't the last."

Nate took a moment to digest that. He regularly guarded people who were in fear for their lives, but they were clients and that was his job. Hearing that someone he cared about had been threatened affected him on a deeper level.

Reading from his notes, Nate ran through personal details he'd learned about the man. "Divorced before his arrest, no children, no living relatives."

"He's had absolutely no visitors since he was incarcerated." Cassie scrolled down the page. "After getting beat up several times, he joined a gang inside the prison for protection."

Sara tapped her pen against her pad. "The only way he could have sent someone after me is if he did it through the gang. I'm not sure the price he'd have to pay for something like that would be worth it to him."

Cassie moved on to the next name. "Brandon Barlow. Sentenced to ten years for violation of a protective order, stalking, assault."

"Stalking?" Nate's eyes widened. "Sounds like he should be at the top of our list."

"I remember him," Sara said. "He was specifically obsessed with his ex-wife."

Nate jotted a note on his Barlow printout before reading from his research. "Aside from the ex-wife and two kids from the marriage, his parents live in an Austin suburb, and he has a brother in that area who's single."

"Next up, David Dillon. Arrested for driving while intoxicated. A search of his vehicle revealed his own personal pharmacy. He had amphetamines, ecstasy, cocaine and enough Oxycodone to make it a first degree felony. It also happened to be his third DWI, making that also a felony under the state's third-strike law." Cassie's lip curled with disgust.

"Sentenced ten months ago to thirty years. He's had several visitors—the most frequent one being his sister,

Joan Dillon. David had no prior arrests, and Joan's record is clean."

"Parents deceased. Sister's his only living relative," Nate added.

"He was the most recent to threaten me when he was sentenced." Sara raised one shoulder in a semi-shrug. "But there were others between Jenkins and Dillon. Guess it comes with the job."

For the next three hours, they repeated the process, sorting the convicts into piles based on their likelihood of being a suspect.

When they finished the last name and slid their piles back into the file folders with the most likely group on top, Sara stretched her arms over her head and sighed. "How did you compile this particular list? I remember the names of some nasty people I prosecuted who weren't included."

"We eliminated everyone who's died." Cassie closed her laptop. "We did extensive research on the ones who've been released from prison. Talked to their parole officers, followed up on their residential situations, jobs, whatever we could find. We made a separate list of those, and a few were in this group." She tapped her folder. "We consider the others unlikely. For now, at least."

"What if this doesn't have anything to do with your job? At least, not with people you sent to prison?" Nate had already discussed this with Cassie, who'd insisted on starting with the convicts. "Was there anyone you worked with who might have a grudge? A coworker who asked you out, and you refused? A defense lawyer who lost to you one too many times?"

Sara pursed her lips as she considered his questions. "I have no idea about defense attorneys. A lot of these trials involved public defenders, and for the most part we keep things civil between us. No one at work wanted to date me that I'm aware of. And the only case that might have inspired jealousy in the other ADAs would have been the murder trial." She scoffed. "If it was that, I'd think they'd have stopped bothering me after Alton took the case for himself."

"But those are all possibilities we should look into." Adam massaged the back of his neck, a habit he had when frustrated or considering a problem. "Sara, you should start a list of every defense attorney you can remember going up against."

"That's easy. My calendar shows dates and attorneys for every trial."

"Perfect." Adam glanced at Cassie. "If we get a list of all employees in that district attorney's office, could you sweet-talk Bishop into using his investigative skills to help us check them all out?"

"There are a lot of employees, especially if you go beyond the assistant DAs and consider legal assistants, clerical staff, everyone else." Sara massaged her forehead. "It would take forever to check them all, and that's if you can even get a list."

"We'll get the list—don't you worry about that. And I'm sure Bishop will be willing to help cull it." Cassie met Sara's gaze. "I know you haven't been dating anyone recently, but I'm going to need a list of everyone you've gone out with for at least the past year."

Sara flicked a quick side-glance at Nate, her cheeks flushed as if she'd just come in from a blizzard. He tried to deny to himself that discussing the men she'd dated bothered him. But it did. Even rationalizing that they both had pasts—and they had no future together—didn't help.

"I'll get with you later on that." Sara's glare at Cassie said a whole lot more than her words.

Must be one hell of a list. His stomach did an unfamiliar flip.

SARA DRAINED HER wine and held out her glass for a refill. They'd come to the Reed ranch straight from the justice building after Adam had suggested grilling steaks for dinner.

"You sure you don't want to wait a few minutes? That one went down pretty fast." Holding the bottle, Nate eyed her like a bartender about to cut her off.

"You're supposed to pour one out for the dead, right? Well, that's what the first glass was. Rest in peace, Sara Bennett." She cocked a brow. "But instead of pouring it out, I poured it in. No sense in wasting good liquor." When Nate still hesitated, she blew out a frustrated breath. "I'm *fine*. And I will drink this next glass slowly and enjoy it as an alive person should."

With a full glass and Nate by her side, Sara wandered out to the patio. The warm weather still held, and she hoped the combination of good weather, food, wine and company would pull her out of her funk.

"You okay?" Cassie asked. "You look a little pale."

"Gotta admit, reading your own obituary in the paper isn't a great way to start the day." Sara dropped onto the patio chair next to Cassie's and set her glass and phone on the side table. "I've had chills before. But this was different—the sensation of rime ice instantly coating my bones, freezing me from the inside out." She wrapped her arms around her, shivering at the memory.

"I can't imagine. But the good news is you're alive." Cassie raised her glass toward Sara. "And I aim to make sure you stay that way."

"Cassie, I need help in the kitchen," Adam called through the back door.

As her friend headed into the house, Sara pondered the possible identity of her stalker. Outrage filled her every time she considered the idea that someone she knew, or at least had crossed paths with, was doing this. If they had an axe to grind with her, they should've had the guts to face her instead of playing this passive-aggressive game.

A few minutes later, Cassie held the door for Adam, who carried a platter loaded with raw steaks. Bishop, who must have just arrived, followed him with a large bowl of what Sara presumed to be veggies.

Cassie reclaimed her chair. "The aroma out here is about to drive you out of your mind."

"I feel useless just sitting here." Sara hated not contributing, but she didn't want to get in the chefs' way. "I'll do the dishes."

"No, you won't." Cassie pointed a finger at Nate. "He will be cleaning up afterward."

"That's the only reason they invited us. So I can do the dishes." Nate rolled his eyes.

"That's the only reason we invited *you*," Adam said. "We invited Sara because we like her."

Despite her head throbbing from anger and frustration, Sara smiled. She was enjoying their easy banter. She would have enjoyed it more without the dark cloud of her own obituary hanging over her. She needed to find the person wreaking havoc on her life.

But just for this evening, she needed serenity. She picked up her glass, kicked off her shoes and strolled across the lawn, scrunching blades of grass between her toes. The feeling took her back to her grandfather's home, where she'd played with abandon in his yard of thick St. Augustine grass.

By the time Sara strolled back to the others with a grin on her face, her stress had pretty much evaporated.

"Feel better?" Nate asked her.

She nodded. "Definitely."

"Y'all better be at the table because everything's almost ready." Adam pulled the steaks from the grill, setting each one on a plate.

Everyone scrambled to the patio table.

"Where are the kids?" Bishop delivered the plates to the table, setting the only one with a fish fillet instead of a steak at his place.

"Still at my mom's." Rachel brought a platter of steaming baked potatoes with her and slid onto her seat. "Brad wanted pizza, and Mom accidentally promised him he could have it. I'll go get them later, unless they crash before I get there. In that case, Mom will be stuck with them all night."

"That might not be a bad thing." Adam waggled his brows at Rachel, who blushed.

"How does someone *accidentally* promise pizza?" Bishop set the bowl of fire-roasted vegetables next to the grilled corn for everyone to share.

Adam laughed. "Have you met Martina?"

"Everything looks amazing." Sara picked up her ear of corn, inhaling the elote seasoning on it. "And I love Mexican street corn." She took a bite, her mouth exploding with flavor.

Nate sat across from her, his eyes crinkling with amusement when she smiled at him. She hadn't noticed his tiny laugh lines before, and she liked them. They made him look more like the fun guy she'd met way back when.

As she had yesterday, Sara felt like she belonged here

with these people. Like part of their extended family. A sense of tranquility settled over her like a warm cloak on a cold night. She joined in on the conversation, enjoyed every morsel of food and got a kick out of Nate's jokes and stories.

But in the back of her mind, she wondered how long this contentment would last.

Chapter Eleven

After several days with no new texts or incidents, Sara began to wonder which was worse: waiting for the other shoe to drop or the shoe actually dropping. The week after Thanksgiving had been quiet, with only a few traffic tickets to deal with. She'd come to the justice center almost every day nonetheless, organizing the filing cabinet and credenza and making the space feel more *hers*.

Now, on this chilly first Monday morning in December, she sat in her chambers reviewing the court docket. An eviction dispute, several DUIs, a few misdemeanor-assault cases from fights at a local bar called the Dead End and an elderly woman who went out in her front yard every full moon, holding her purse open and calling out "Fill 'er up" while turning in circles. Unfortunately she did it buck naked, and her neighbors had finally had enough. Not exactly the felonies Sara hoped to preside over someday as a district court judge. But at least some of them were…intriguing.

Nate, sitting in a visitor's chair and tapping away on his laptop, had already cleared the courtroom and left the bailiff standing guard inside the entrance. He glanced up and caught her watching him. "What?"

"Just curious if anyone's catching your attention on there." She tipped her head toward his computer. Cassie had received the list of the DA's Office employees from Austin several days ago, and they were working their way through it with hopes one name would pop off the page and this nightmare would be over.

"Nothing yet." He tapped his thumbs on the chair's arms.

"I wish I could've helped more." The entire list had been given to Sara first. Her job had been to review every name, looking for anyone who might've had an issue with her. She hadn't found any, so Cassie had then divided it between herself, her brothers and Bishop so they could research each employee. "It'll be a waste of so much time if he isn't even on that list."

"But worth the time if he is," Nate said. "And in the meantime, Cassie and Adam are also doing deep dives into the most likely criminal prospects."

A staccato knock sounded against the door, and Nate crossed the room and cracked it just enough to see who it was before backing up and opening it for Lorinda, Sara's judicial assistant, to enter.

"Sorry to interrupt." The woman walked briskly to her boss's desk and held out a small manila envelope. "This just came for you."

As Sara reached to take it, Nate barked out a sharp, "No!"

Sara jerked back her hand as if she'd burned it, and the assistant froze in place, her mouth and eyes wide. After pulling two tissues from the box on her desk, Nate used them to take the envelope from Lorinda without directly touching it.

"Didn't mean to scare you, but we don't know what might be in it." Nate set it on a side table across the room. "Do you have any latex gloves?"

"Judge Harmon always kept a box of them in our storage closet in case anyone brought evidence in here." Lorinda disappeared in a blur.

Sara joined Nate. "You think it's a letter bomb or anthrax or something?"

"I'm not taking any chances." He met her eyes. "Why don't you step into your restroom and close the door?"

"Nate—"

"Please don't fight me on this. Just let me do my job."

Lorinda returned, handed him the box of gloves and what looked like a small portable scanner on the desk. "This is letter-bomb detector. Judge Harmon requisitioned it a while back, but we've never used it."

She showed Nate how it worked, then skedaddled out of the office and closed the door behind her. Nate donned a pair of the gloves, and Sara retreated into her private bathroom before she had to be told again.

Sara closed her eyes, held her breath and murmured a prayer that Nate didn't die while protecting her. Unable to hear anything through the closed door, her mind sought out every conceivable tragedy that might be happening to him.

She was about to crack open the door and take a peek when Nate called to her, "It's safe to come out."

"Was it anything deadly?" she asked.

"I'm not sure what it is." Nate glanced up from what looked like pictures in his hands. "There was a small rip in the envelope, so I used that to confirm there were no powders inside. The scanner showed no explosives, so I opened it up without compromising the adhesive, labels or stamps."

Sara stood next to him and looked at the pictures of an older man as Nate flipped through them. The man leaving a house, coming out of a store, sitting in a diner.

"Let me see those," she said, grabbing his arm.

Nate held them out of her reach. "Put on gloves first. We may be able to get fingerprints off them."

Her hands damp with sweat, she forced them into gloves

and grabbed the pack of pictures. A gasp escaped her as her stomach took a nosedive. She studied the envelope. No return address, but it had been postmarked in Cooley, Texas. Her legs turned to rubber, and she collapsed onto the closest chair.

Nate dropped to a knee in front of her. "What is it? Do you know the man in those pictures?"

Her mouth was as dry as the Chihuahuan Desert, and she could only nod for a moment. With the pictures gripped in one hand, she took hold of Nate's arm with the other, her nails digging into his skin. But he didn't even flinch. Just waited her out until she could find her voice.

"It's my grandfather." Sara's throat threatened to close again, and she gasped for air. "And the envelope was mailed from Cooley, Texas, where he lives."

NATE STOOD IN the middle of his sister's office, listening to his siblings' discussion. As soon as they'd realized her grandfather was being targeted, Sara had asked Lorinda to reschedule today's court cases. Then he'd rushed Sara to the sheriff's department within the justice center. Cassie, Adam, Noah and Bree had joined them to hash out the best plan going forward.

Cassie paced from her desk to the window and back. "I can call the Hudson County Sheriff and ask him to provide protection for your grandfather."

"I don't like the idea of leaving his safety in the hands of a stranger." Sara shook her head. "And knowing Pops, he'd tell the sheriff he's fine on his own."

"The only other option is to have him come here," Adam said.

"Yes! I'd feel much better if he were here with me. Except we'd have the same problem. Pops will blow off the potential for danger and stay in Cooley." Sara's gaze roamed across each face in the room, coming to rest on Nate's. "Unless someone goes there and brings him back."

Silence reigned for a moment while everyone's eyes turned to Nate.

"Why are you all looking at me? My job is to keep Sara safe, and I can't do that if I'm three hundred miles away."

"Closer to two hundred." Noah cringed a little when Nate spun toward him. "Maybe two twenty-five?"

Sara stepped closer to him. "Please, Nate? I know he'll be safe with you."

He didn't like this plan. He didn't leave the side of someone he was protecting until the job was finished. And catching Sara's stalker was far from over.

"The only reason I asked you to keep Sara safe was because she didn't want us hanging around her all day and drawing attention." Cassie raised one brow in that big-sister I'm-in-charge look that Nate hated. "But that won't be an issue today. You'll be gone half a day at most. We'll keep her right here in my office until you return with her grandfather. One of us will be with her the entire time."

But cool fingers of reason coiled around his arm, halting him. "Please, Nate." The pleading look on Sara's face damn near ripped his guts out.

Pale blue eyes that normally sparkled were now dull with worry, her face drawn and colorless. With nothing more than a look passing between them, his fury hardened into stone-cold resolve. Whatever it took to end the madness of this stalker, he'd do it.

Whatever it took.

Because when he gazed down into those anguish-filled eyes, everything faded away except one inevitable reality— he would face down the very demons from hell if it made Sara Bennett happy again.

"All right, I'll do it. I'll get your grandfather and bring him here to you. Okay?"

Tears of what he hoped was relief rolled down her ashen cheeks as she nodded.

"Good. Now, the pictures the stalker took are from a distance, so why don't you give me a good description of your grandfather."

Sara recovered quickly. She brushed away her tears, glancing around as if embarrassed in front of the others. "He's tall, about six-three. And broad." She held her hands out on either side of her shoulders. "He's developed a bit of a beer belly since he retired, but don't ever mention I told you that. It's a sensitive subject."

Nate cracked a small grin. "I'm sure I can avoid bringing it up in conversation." That was the easiest promise he'd made in days.

"Basically, he's a larger-than-life pillar of dignity in snakeskin boots and a Stetson." She smiled back. "You two will get along great."

SARA WAS ON the phone to her grandfather as soon as Nate agreed to go get him. "Hi, Pops."

"Well, I'll be. And here I was, just thinking about you. Guess we've still got that Bennett mind-mojo going for us." His cheerful voice made her smile, despite the situation. "How's life down there in Boone County?"

Pops had been the first one she'd told, after Cassie, about moving to Resolute.

"I'm fine for the moment, but something alarming has been happening in my life, and I'm worried it might have spilled over into yours."

"Tell me what's going on." Her grandfather's tone changed to one of concern.

"It seems I have a stalker. Don't get upset—I'm okay. Cassie's brother Nate is a bodyguard, and he's been protecting me." As Sara filled him in, she massaged her forehead, dreading what she had to tell him next. "The thing is, we think he's been watching you, too. I received an envelope of pictures this morning. Pictures of you, your house. Nate's going to fly up there this afternoon and bring you back here so he can protect you, too."

"Hold on now, kiddo. These days, dirtbags like that can pull pictures from the internet and alter them digitally. I've seen the technique used before in intimidation schemes. Besides, this old man can take care of himself." His attempt at reassuring her fell flat.

Having a strong-willed, independent grandfather would make it difficult for her to convince him, but she had to make him understand the danger. She'd have to tread lightly, however. Pops didn't like being told what to do.

"The pictures were dated the day before yesterday. Can you remember what shirt you had on then?"

"Let me think." Pops paused. "Hmm, wasn't a shirt. It's been cool lately, so I was wearing my new green sweater. A pullover. First time I've worn it, and let me tell you, it's softer than a baby's backside."

Sara swallowed past a tightness in her throat. "With a shawl collar? Just enough of a V-neck to reveal your white undershirt beneath it?"

There was a long, drawn-out silence as Pops processed the information. "I'd rather you keep that bodyguard close to you. I'll call a couple buddies at the police department, ask them to do drive-bys of my house." He chuckled but the sound lacked the rich timbre of genuine amusement. "Give them something to do besides writing traffic tickets. Anyway, you know I don't much like to travel these days."

"Pops, the sheriff's department is treating this very seri-ously. They believe it's a credible threat, as well as a danger-ous one. I'm afraid having a couple of local police buddies do a few drive-bys isn't going to cut it." Sara's voice shook from pent-up fear, and she paused to take a calming breath. Without a doubt, Pops was the single most important per-son in her life, and to lose him…

With her eyes burning from unshed tears and her voice continuing to quaver, she decided to change tactics and ap-peal directly to his heartstrings. "I couldn't live with my-self if anything happened to you. You get that, don't you?"

Sara let her plea sink in and then hit her grandfather with a one-two sucker punch. Deliberately pushing away her fear, she replaced it with the full force of her determination to keep the one person who'd always been there for her safe. "I understand that you're not going to like hearing this," she said, using the stern, no-nonsense tone she used as a judge when passing down a sentence, "but I'm not asking you to come here. I'm telling you. Nate Reed will be coming to get you, so pack a bag. I've given him your cell number, and he'll be texting you with the details."

Then, to soften the sting of her harshly delivered de-mand, she repeated words of affection they had shared since she'd been a small girl: "I love you all the way up to the highest sky, all the way down to the deepest sea."

Her grandfather blew out a heavy breath. "Damn, you drive a hard bargain, but if it'll let you rest easier, I'll do it. You know I'd do anything for you."

Relief flooded her. "I do, so I have one last favor to ask. Let one of those police buddies of yours drive you to the airport, okay? Just to be on the safe side?"

"Can't wait to see the looks on their faces when I request

a chauffeur." His chuckle was genuine this time and drew a small smile from her in return.

"See you soon, Pops. I love you."

"Love you more, kiddo."

AN HOUR LATER, Nate jogged onto the tarmac at Victoria Regional Airport, where a twin-turboprop Beechcraft waited for him. He believed his siblings would do everything in their power to keep Sara safe. But he had no intention of being away from her any longer than necessary.

He'd called in a favor from country-music superstar Byron Cain, whose home was in Texas when he wasn't touring the country or recording in California. A few years back, Nate had helped Cain extricate himself from a particularly volatile situation, and the star had been more than happy to let Nate use his private aircraft in return for the favor.

As Nate closed the distance to the plane, a stout December gust ripped at his windbreaker, and he cursed himself for not wearing a heavier jacket. At least his military-grade sunglasses cut the midday sun's glare, for which he was grateful. In his line of business, even one moment of blindness could mean the difference between life and death.

He stopped before a man shading his eyes with one hand and holding the other outstretched.

"Jack Palmquist." The man shouted to be heard over the mechanical sound of the whirling engines. "I'll be your pilot today. It may be cold, but the weather's clear and we'll have a tailwind on the way. We should make good time."

Nate shook his hand. "Nate Reed. What does 'good time' mean?" He climbed aboard, the pilot following and securing the door before taking his seat.

Jack pulled out a navigation map. "Cooley Municipal

Airport is about two hundred miles away as the crow flies. Best guess, we should arrive in about an hour, give or take."

"Sounds good."

"And since it's just you, feel free to sit up front if you like."

Nate hesitated, about to refuse. He had no desire to talk, but the waterways, wooded hills and limestone canyons of the Texas Hill Country would be spectacular. "Thanks. I will."

Turned out, Jack was a decent flying companion. Other than discussing a few logistics, he remained silent for the entire hour and ten minutes it took until they landed and taxied up to the terminal.

"I understand this is a round trip. We'll be returning to Victoria?"

"Yes. As soon as possible."

"All right. I'll go ahead and file my fight plan. Mr. Cain said I was at your disposal, so I'll be right here, ready and waiting, whenever you need to leave."

Again, Nate reached out and shook the man's hand. "Appreciate it. Um, Mr. Cain did mention to you that I would be picking up a passenger here, right?"

"Yes, sir, he did."

"Good. I don't anticipate this taking long. The man I'm meeting is supposed to be here already."

"As I said, ready and waiting."

Nate opened the door, stepped from the wing to the ground and jogged several yards to the small but well-appointed terminal. Clean carpet, plush lounge chairs and tables holding a spread of magazines.

Only one other person was there, a man sitting behind a tall counter with a computer and phone to his right, a scale to weigh luggage on his left. The man—Alan, according to his name badge—was short, thin and maybe midforties. Definitely not the description Sara had given him of her grandfather when the whole family had been arguing about who should go get the retired judge.

Alan looked up from the magazine he'd been reading. "Can I help you?"

"I'm looking for Archer Bennett. He was supposed to meet me here."

"Judge Bennett called me, said he'd be fifteen minutes late."

"How long ago did he call you?"

"About half an hour or so. But the judge lives a decent stretch outside of town on the far side. And then there's the train. Get stuck at one of the crossings, and it's anybody's guess how long you could be sitting there." He shook his head slowly. "'Specially if they start switching cars to a sidetrack and disconnecting them."

Afraid he'd develop a tic in his eye if he listened to much more, Nate wandered over to a wall of windows near the front door.

Cassie had planned on calling in a favor for the police escort, but Judge Bennett had told her not to bother, as he and the chief were old friends. And exactly forty-six excruciating minutes later, a Cooley PD cruiser blazed into the parking lot and a uniformed officer stepped out. He rounded the car and opened the passenger door, holding it for a man who fit the description of Sara's grandfather right down to the snakeskin boots.

Archer—wearing a pair of pressed blue jeans, a Western shirt with a black bolo tie secured with a silver Lone Star slide and a leather jacket—went to the trunk and pulled out a suitcase. Then he headed into the terminal.

"This man is waiting for you, Judge." Alan motioned toward Nate.

"Sorry I'm late," Bennett said. "Damn train. Nothing to do but wait the thing out."

"That's what I told him," Alan said. "Said it was probably a train."

"And you were right on the money." Bennett winked at him, then turned again to Nate. "I take it you're here for my protection, son."

He held out his hand. "Nate Reed."

Bennett gripped it tightly and shook with strength. "Judge Archer Bennett, but you can call me Archer. And son, I'm notifying you that I'm carrying."

Nate knew he was being sized up and shook the man's hand with equal force. "You're permitted to bring your weapon on board, sir, but it needs to be unloaded and safely stowed."

"I am well aware of the law. It's packed in a locked gun case in my luggage, unloaded."

They headed out the glass doors to the Beechcraft, where Jack was finishing his preflight checklist. Nate climbed onto the wing and held the door open for the judge, who crawled in with his suitcase.

Nate followed him in, and they buckled themselves into rear seats while Jack settled into the pilot's seat.

"Archer, this is our pilot, Jack Palmquist."

The two men exchanged greetings, then Jack started the engines. Once the twin props sputtered to life, they taxied toward the runway. Ten minutes later they were airborne. The passenger area was comfortable, and it didn't take Archer long to locate the liquor bottles and glasses. He helped himself to three fingers of whiskey and offered to pour one for Nate, who refused.

He refused because he was working and needed to keep his wits about him. He was now responsible for keeping two people safe instead of one. And with no idea if the stalker was still in Cooley or back in Resolute, Nate had to be ready for anything.

"One of the nice things about being retired is that every hour is cocktail hour." The judge took a sip and released a happy sigh. "Now, son, my granddaughter filled me in on what's generally been happening, but I want to hear it from you."

Sara had told him her grandfather would pester everyone until he had all the details, so it was best to just get it all out there from the get-go. Nate spent the next twenty minutes going over everything that had happened to date. Well, everything stalker related.

"So, what does this bastard want from my granddaughter?"

"That's the frustrating thing. The text messages, the obit, even the threat to you have come with no demands, no motives. No 'do this or else.' My sister and her deputies are leaving no stone unturned in their search for the perp."

Archer sipped his drink. "Can you tell me if she's considered giving up the judgeship and going back to the Austin DA's office?"

"Wouldn't make a difference if she did. The texts started coming before she accepted the position in Resolute." Nate's voice filled with respect. "And I get the impression once she makes a commitment, she sticks to it. I'd be surprised if anything could drive her back to Austin before the election for a new judge in a few months."

"Pleased to hear that. Not about the texts—about the timing. I know full well that girl took this job to make me happy. Thinks that by becoming a judge, she'll be honoring me. Which is a big load of bullpucky. Hell, I'd be proud no matter what profession she chose. But she was always so enthusiastic about my work, and I didn't want to discourage any of her interests. Especially after what she endured."

In the bodyguard racket, Nate had learned early on not to pry. Detachment was key. But with Sara, he'd already crossed so many lines. So he urged Archer to continue. "Endured?"

"From my good-for-nothing son and his wife, the trust-fund baby. The two people who should have loved that girl the most. All she ever got from them was indifference or derision. Turned her into a timid mouse with their neglect." Archer's gaze seemed to shift inward, sadness pulling the corners of his mouth down. "Whatever spunk Sara has now was hard-won on her own behalf."

Nate saw regret on the old man's face, but he saw pride, too.

"I did what I could. Hell, I kept her almost every summer. She'd sit in court most days during the week. No life for a child, but she said she loved it." A gravelly chuckle came from deep within his chest. "When she got to be old enough to leave home alone, she wasn't having it. Still insisted on coming to the courthouse with me. Day in, day out, year after year." He looked Nate straight in the eye. "I love that girl like nobody's business, and I won't stand for someone tormenting her. You Reeds going to get this bastard?"

"Yes, sir, we are."

"That's exactly what I wanted to hear." Archer tossed back the rest of his drink, then watched the scenery below as they traveled back to Sara.

Chapter Twelve

"Pops texted that they just landed in Victoria," Sara announced to Cassie as she slid her phone back into her pocket and exhaled an afternoon's worth of anxiety. "They'll come straight here."

From the time Nate had left to get her grandfather, she'd been in either Cassie's or Adam's office, depending on which one was babysitting her at the time. Not that her friends used that term, but it was how she felt. Cassie even accompanied her to the sheriff's "private" restroom because it was actually a public one she'd commandeered with a sign and a lock.

Cassie, still researching possible stalker suspects, looked up from her computer. "I'm glad they made it back safely. Maybe now you can stop staring out my office window and sit down."

Taking one of the visitor chairs, Sara stretched out her legs and watched Cassie squint at one monitor, look at another one as if cross-checking information, then jot down notes. She'd only seen her friend a few times over the years—always when Cassie had come to Austin on business—but their friendship had been maintained through frequent phone calls. Catching up on work, agreeing that relationships were a time suck and more trouble than they were worth, sharing news about the people in their lives.

Although they'd definitely enjoyed themselves in college, they had both been serious students, working much harder than they'd played. It seemed the trend had continued as they pursued their careers. The two small frown lines between Cassie's brows never completely disappeared these days. Sara self-consciously smoothed the area at the top of her own nose with a finger, wondering if the same was true for her.

Even so, she had to give it to her friend—Cassie looked younger and happier now than the last time they'd seen each other. And Sara bet Bishop deserved the credit for that.

A knock sounded, and Cassie went to the door. "Who is it?"

"Adam."

"What's the password?"

"Very funny. Open the door."

"That's not the password. You can try again after twenty seconds."

Heavy footsteps faded away, and Cassie laughed. "His sense of humor is still a work in progress."

She'd just returned to her chair when a quick rap sounded before a key turned in the lock. Helen cracked open the door and peeked in, a stern look on her face. "Did you tell Adam I should give him *my* key to your office? You know I don't—"

"Allow anyone to touch your keys." Adam pushed the door in and stepped around Helen. "Yes, we know that. I apologize for lying, but thank you for getting me in here."

Cassie gasped. "You *lied* to Helen?"

The older woman straightened her back, pushed her glasses up on her nose and snorted. "I don't have time for this nonsense. And you're too old for these games, Adam

Reed." She pulled the door shut behind her with more force than necessary.

Cassie and Adam stared at each before cracking up.

"I can't believe you did that." Cassie did a little snort-laugh that made Sara join in.

"Password?" Adam rolled his eyes as he took a seat.

Sara's phone chimed with a text, and as with the earlier one, her stomach clenched until she saw it was from her grandfather. "They're about ten minutes out, and he says Nate wants Adam downstairs by the time they park."

"*Who* says?" Adam glanced at her, brows raised.

"My grandfather. He texted me when they landed, and now they're almost here."

"Your grandfather texts?" Adam stood. "That's cool."

"What? You sound surprised that someone over seventy can text." Sara feigned outrage. "Why, Adam, is that age-ism I detect?"

Adam's posture stiffened and his jaw muscles flexed. "No, no. Nothing like that." He turned toward the door. "It's just, I was thinking about Judge Harmon, who refused to join the technical revolution. I guess what I'm trying to say is I'm impressed."

"Uh-huh."

"I'll be downstairs." He fled the office, but not before making sure they were locked in safely behind him.

"He didn't even say why he came in here in the first place. You really shouldn't tease my poor brother like that."

Rolling her eyes, Sara said, "Don't you start being a stick-in-the-mud, too." She hadn't realized how much she'd missed their good-natured bantering that had been commonplace when they were college roommates.

Cassie's attempt at a steely expression dissolved into laughter. "Told you his sense of humor isn't fully developed."

"Well, if he's impressed my grandfather can text, Adam's in for a big surprise when he meets the man in person." Sara scoffed. "Pops only retired at seventy-five because it's the mandatory age for judges. But he's never slowed down."

"I only met him briefly at graduation, but you're right— he's going to redefine grandfathers for Adam." Cassie left her desk to look out her window. "And speaking of Pops…"

"They're here?" Sara crossed the room and stood next to Cassie.

With her heavy caseload at the DA's office, she hadn't visited Pops in months. To see him here, safe and sound, brightened what had been a long, fretful day. He appeared strong and imposing as he climbed out of the pickup, and she knew when he shook Adam's hand that Pops's firm grip had plenty of muscle behind it. *I bet you're impressed now, Chief Deputy Reed.*

As Adam had approached the passenger side of the truck, Nate rounded the back of it and stood behind her grandfather, the two brothers guarding him from all sides. The final threads of fear that had tied her in knots all day finally snapped.

It was one thing for her to feel secure in Nate's protection. But to watch him in action, his head on a swivel as he propelled her grandfather up the justice center's steps and to safety, filled her with admiration and gratitude and some other feeling she couldn't put a name to and didn't have time to figure out because her Pops was walking in the door.

"There's my girl." Her grandfather met her halfway across the office, his arms held wide to scoop her into a bear hug.

"Pops! I'm so glad you're here." Sara allowed the hug to continue longer than normal because she knew he was as worried about her as she was him.

He finally released her and held her at arm's length. "Let me take a look at you, *Judge* Sara Bennett. These people taking good care of you?"

"Of course they are." She grabbed Cassie's hand and pulled her next to her. "You remember Cassie?"

"'Course I do." He tipped his head to the side and squinted. "But she's a mite more intimidating in that sheriff's uniform than she was in a graduation cap and gown."

Cassie smiled. "Nice to see you again, Judge Bennett. I hope your trip was uneventful."

"Gonna tell you all this one time and one time only. Call me Archer. I believe two Judge Bennetts in the same town will only confuse us all." He winked at Sara. "And yes, my trip was indeed uneventful. Would've been downright boring if I hadn't had Nate here to talk to the whole way."

Her grandfather gave her a stern look, and Sara shot a questioning glance at Nate as her cheeks began to heat. But his blank expression gave nothing away.

"I hear tell you blew up my gavel. That true?"

Although relieved he wasn't asking about Nate, Sara was heartbroken about destroying the gavel. "I'm sorry, Pops. If I'd had any idea—"

Her grandfather chuckled. "That chunk of wood's best days were in the rearview mirror long before I gave it to you. I'll get you a new one, inscribed with a special message. Best way for a judge to start their career."

Then he turned and looked each Reed in the eye. "So, what's the plan?"

AFTER A LOW-KEY law enforcement escort to the mansion, Sara stood in the foyer with her grandfather while Nate checked the house.

"Well, if this don't beat all." Pops meandered over to the staircase and grabbed the banister, trying to shake it. "The house may be old, but it's got good bones."

"And updated plumbing, thank God." Sara smiled. "It's taken some getting used to. But I still miss my condo."

Pops dismissed her words with a wave of his hand. "I never did think that hoity-toity penthouse was the right fit for you. Seemed more like someplace your mother would live."

Comparing Sara's choice of a home to her mother's lifestyle was an uncharacteristic comment for Pops to make, and the hurt she felt must have shown on her face.

"Sorry about that." He smoothed his bushy white mustache with his thumb and forefinger. "Guess the way they raised you has been on my mind lately."

Nate came down the stairs. "Everything's fine." His glance bounced from one Bennett to the other, maybe sensing the tension between them. "I'm going to scan the security footage while you two catch up."

Sara led her grandfather to a guest room on the second floor. "Do you need help settling in?"

"I travel light." Archer hoisted the bag in his hand, then set it by the bed. "But I could use a good cup of coffee."

Sara wrapped an arm around the old man's waist and leaned into him. "That I can get you."

With a mug of coffee in Pops's hand and an espresso in Sara's, they made themselves comfortable in the parlor. Well, as comfortable as one could be sitting on a stiff horsehair sofa. She would have preferred the upholstered chairs in the dining room, but she wanted to stay out of Nate's earshot. Pops's voice could carry, and she had no idea what direction the conversation might take.

Her grandfather looked like a lumberjack in a tea shop as he searched for a place to set his mug. Sara saw a stack of glass coasters across the room and retrieved two for the side tables next to them.

Pops rested his hands on his knees. "I will say, you might want to see about some furniture more appropriate to this century."

Sara laughed. "I'm working on it. But I can't go overboard. I'll only be here a few months, just until Judge Harmon's term is up."

Pops's bushy brows headed for his hairline. "And then what?"

"Back home." She shrugged.

"Why are you so hell-bent to get back to Austin? I've never understood the attraction it holds for you." He sipped his coffee.

"It's where my life is." Smiling, she added, "And after I'm done here, maybe I'll have a better shot at becoming a district judge up there."

"Sara, I appreciate you wanting to follow in my footsteps. But you don't have to be a judge to make me proud of you." His blue eyes, almost as pale as hers, shined with tenderness. "I just want you to be happy doing whatever it is you love."

Folding one leg beneath her, Sara turned sideways on the couch to face her grandfather. "But I *am*. I love the judicial system." She took one of his hands, covered with prominent veins and age spots, in hers. "But I never wanted to become a judge *for* you. I want to be one *because* of you."

His brows pulled together like two caterpillars about to do battle. "Why don't you do an old man a favor and explain the difference."

"I've always wanted to make you proud of me, no matter what I did. And that's because I respect you so much—as a judge and as an honorable man. The summers I spent with you were my best childhood memories, and during those times I learned about ethics and morals and the difference a person can make when they live by their principles." She leaned forward and kissed his leathery cheek. "*That's* why I wanted to be a judge."

Pops ducked his head away from her and swiped at his eye. "You people ever dust in here? Something's making my eyes itch."

Sara kept a straight face. "I never dust in here. It gives my guests an excuse to cry without getting embarrassed."

At that, Pops straightened, scrubbed his hands across his face and chuckled. "I must be getting soft in my old age."

"You?" She shook her head. "Never."

"You mean the world to me, kiddo."

"The feeling's mutual." She took a sip of her cooling espresso. "So, you ready for dinner?"

"I just need to get one thing straight."

"Yes?" *Please don't let him ask if there's anything going on between Nate and me.*

"If you've always wanted to be a judge, regardless of the reason why, and you're now a judge, why give it up when the term's over? Why not run for the position?"

"Because I'm not a district judge, and this isn't Travis County." Sara sighed. "And like I said earlier, I enjoy living in Austin."

"Hmm. So being a rural county judge isn't good enough? You want to be more important than that?"

"That's not what I said."

"Sorry—I must have misunderstood." Pops stood, mug

of coffee in hand. "Just do me one favor, okay? While you're here, take a good look around."

"At what?"

But instead of answering, he headed toward the kitchen, leaving her to wonder what pearl of wisdom she had just missed.

Chapter Thirteen

Despite Nate's suggestion that court be postponed for another day or more, he'd been overruled. Sara hadn't wanted
the arraignments to get even more backed up than they were
after the Thanksgiving-week holiday and the Pops Express
trip yesterday.

And Pops had insisted on seeing her in action on the bench
while he was here. The general consensus was that the Boone
County judicial system would not be held hostage by Sara's
stalker.

The last case of the day was the naked moon worshipper,
and that one moved more quickly than expected since Sara
refused to view the footage brought in by the neighbors.
The woman agreed to wear clothes in the future or stick to
her backyard. With that, Tuesday was a wrap.

While they waited in Sara's chambers for her to freshen
up in her private bathroom, Nate turned to Archer. "What
did you see outside the diner last night?"

The three of them had gone to the Busy B for dinner the
previous evening, as Archer had been craving chicken-fried
steak. Nate, sitting across from Sara and her grandfather,
had noticed the old man sneaking furtive glances through
the diner's front window.

"That obvious, huh?" Archer smoothed his mustache.

"Just thought someone passing by looked familiar, but it was probably nothing."

"Brown jacket, ball cap pulled low on his forehead?"

Archer's eyes widened. "You don't miss a thing, do you?"

"Wouldn't be very good at my job if I did." Nate glanced at the closed powder-room door. "Where'd you recognize him from?"

"I didn't get a good look at his face, so I'm not sure." He shrugged. "It was more just a feeling, like I'd seen someone move the same way, walk with a similar gait."

Nate had spent enough time with Archer Bennett over the past two days to realize he was an intelligent man with good instincts. And the old man would never put his granddaughter at risk. So Nate wouldn't push him just yet on who he thought he'd seen.

Sara stepped into the room. "I'm glad you were here for today's cases, Pops, and not the one I had a couple weeks ago. Live geese took over the courtroom."

"It was a joy to watch you dispensing justice, my girl." Archer's chest visibly swelled. "But I bet the geese were something to see."

"I can laugh about it now, but at the time…" She shook her head. "We ready to head home?"

"We've just been waiting for you." Nate finally pulled his gaze from her, no easy task when she was glowing with happiness. *Her grandfather brings that out in her.* A tiny prickle of envy toward the old man stung him.

They walked down the steps of the justice center, Nate looking around for possible threats.

Archer paused. "Nice little town you got here. That town square across the way is special. Gives the place a real down-home feeling. I'd like to get a picture or two while we're here."

Uncomfortable with them dawdling out in the open, Nate

opened his mouth to urge them into his truck. But at the last second, he stopped himself. Something didn't ring true with this scenario. They'd already given Archer the fifty-cent tour of Resolute, and he hadn't stopped once for a picture.

Catching the sly look Archer aimed at him, Nate did another visual sweep of the area. Scanning the town square, he caught sight of the brown-jacketed man from outside the diner last night. Although his pulse jumped, Nate's eyes moved past the man as if he were nothing more than a light post.

The judge fished his phone from his jacket pocket and fiddled with it before aiming it past the corner of the town square toward some shops, as a tourist might do.

Nate's phone chirped, and he ignored it.

"Aren't you gonna get that, son? Might be something important."

Nate's siblings came down the front steps and joined them as he checked his messages.

Brown jacket park bench. Saw him outside my house in Cooley.

Nate forwarded the text to his siblings, then stepped closer to Archer. Pointing down the street as if at something of interest, he asked, "You sure?"

"As sure as cornbread goes with greens."

Sara stepped closer. "Will someone tell me what the hell is going on?" Her voice was low.

Archer put his arm around his granddaughter's shoulders. "Just look at my phone like I'm showing you pictures." He pointed to the screen, and she nodded. "There's a guy in the park across the street who was outside my house a few days ago and outside the diner last night."

Sara's head jerked up, but before she could look toward the town square Archer whispered into her ear, and she focused on his phone again.

Nate pointed at the justice center's facade. "While you two pretend to take pictures of the building, make your way up the steps to the door."

Cassie nodded and laughed as if someone had made a joke, then spoke softly. "Nate, you go straight at him. Adam will circle around and come in from the north side of the square. I'll come from the east. Everyone watch for weapons." She glanced at Noah. "You stay with Sara and Archer, and as soon as we make our move, get them back inside." She walked toward her SUV, calling over her shoulder, "See you tomorrow."

Adam followed on her heels, heading for his vehicle.

Archer bellowed to Nate, "Son, I want a photo of my granddaughter and me at the top of the steps."

Noah followed them, standing just out of frame, as he would if they were really taking pictures. Nate backed up into the street, facing the justice center, pretending to do the old man's bidding. When the text popped up that Adam and Cassie were in position, Nate continued to hold up his phone as if snapping photos of Archer and Sara. But he'd flipped the camera around so he could watch the man in the brown jacket behind him.

No longer sitting on the bench, the man now leaned against a tree, splitting his attention between the picture-taking scene in front of him and his own phone.

While Archer and Sara changed poses, Nate waited until his siblings eased into his selfie screen. Then he shoved his phone into his jeans pocket, turned and ran toward the town square.

Startled like the proverbial deer, the man froze. Only for

a second, but it was enough time for Nate to almost reach him. And when the stranger finally snapped out of it, he took off like a lightning flash, beelining directly for Cassie.

The head-on collision was avoided at the last moment when the man jerked sideways, pivoting into the landscaped areas and hotfooting it like his heels were ablaze.

Damn, he's fast.

Nate signaled Adam, each rounding on him from a different direction, but the guy ran like a world-class sprinter. Cassie circled back and joined in the chase as they left the square and tore down Main Street.

Nate saw the brown jacket whip around a corner a half block ahead. "Cut him off!" he yelled, waving his arms to indicate the direction.

Cassie angled left and headed for the next parallel street. As Nate started to round the corner, Cassie, running past the far end of the block, motioned for him to keep going on Main. At the next intersection, Adam peeled off onto the cross street while Nate continued east.

Passing the next alley, Nate saw a flash of movement and charged. The man was tiring. Nate gained precious inches on their person of interest. The man looked over his shoulder, slowing him down more. Nate surged forward, reached out his hand.

So close.

He leaped, yelling as the breeze sailed through his hair. For a second, he thought he'd come up empty. But at the last second, his arms wrapped around the man's torso, and he took him down.

As a painful expulsion of breath came from the man, Nate silently thanked him for cushioning his own fall. Unable to struggle, the man gaped like a fish out of water, desperately seeking oxygen. Nate pulled the man's arm behind his back and slid his own through it, putting pressure on both the elbow and shoulder at once.

All the suspect could do was lie face down, groaning. Each time he tried to pull loose, Nate tweaked his grip, shutting all movement down.

Cassie and Adam converged on them from opposite ends of the alley.

Panting, Cassie pulled cuffs from her belt bag, then paused. "How are you keeping him pinned like that? It looks like you're barely holding him down."

Nate smiled up at her. Technique.

"I want to arrange for you to teach a class on that to my department." She cuffed the man's loose arm to the one Nate held, then sat him against the wall.

"Be happy to, sis."

"Want me to call for a car?" Adam asked.

Still out of breath, Cassie nodded. "I'm not taking any chances by walking this guy all the way back." While Adam radioed the office, she looked at Nate. "See how much fun you've been missing out on by not becoming a deputy? With four Reeds on the force, no criminal would dare set foot in Boone County."

"Nice try." Nate tipped his head toward the restrained man. "You got this?"

"Of course. Go on, check on your *client*."

He didn't need to be told twice. Getting a second wind, he jogged back toward the justice center. If this was their guy, Nate would finally be able to tell Sara that she was safe. The dark circles under her eyes would disappear and he'd once again see that dazzling smile of hers.

Then an ache in his chest slowed his pace, and he wondered what a heart attack felt like. But he knew this pain wasn't that.

If Sara was safe, she would no longer need a bodyguard. It would be time for him to leave for California.

LESS THAN AN hour later Nate stood in the small observation area, scowling at their runner through the thick one-way glass of the interrogation room. It appeared they had their guy. That should have set him at ease, but he couldn't shake the feeling that something wasn't right. It didn't help that his body confirmed his apprehension, remaining stiff, his muscles knotted with tension. "So, you're sure. You've never seen this guy before?"

Standing beside him, Sara crossed her arms over her chest, her hands holding her upper arms as if she were cold. Although physically safe at the moment, her cocooned stance told Nate fear still controlled her mind. And yet he couldn't bring himself to comfort her. He'd be leaving soon, and it was time to start separating business from pleasure. Go back to the way things should have been all along. Detached. Professional.

She shook her head. "Never."

Her brows furrowed as she watched Cassie and Noah enter the interrogation room. Harsh fluorescent lights illuminated four walls covered in gunmetal-gray paint, chipped and dingy. In the center of the room, two metal chairs sat on one side of a scarred metal table that was bolted to the floor. The runner sat on the opposite side, his hands free, but a handcuff bar attached to the table was ready in case the need arose. A camera was mounted on one wall, high in the corner.

Cassie stood back as Noah sat opposite the subject, handed him a plastic bottle of water and opened a folder.

Why let Noah have the lead?

This wasn't like Cassie at all, particularly on such a notable case. His sister was a take-charge kind of person, had been her whole life. Adam had been talking up Noah's performance of late, especially since he and Bree had cracked the meth-ring case. Still, it was hard for Nate to ignore years of memories concerning his twin's antics.

"This interview is being recorded. This is Deputy Sheriff Noah Reed. Also present is Sheriff Cassie Reed. Now then, sir, I need your name for our records."

A microphone carried Noah's voice into the observation area. His timbre was firm, the kind of tone that brooked no nonsense. Nate decided he would just have to trust Cassie to know what she was doing with regards to Noah.

The perp's dark, limp hair was plastered to his head with dried sweat. His stubbly chin hardened with hostility. "Am I under arrest?"

"Not yet." Noah rested his forearms on the table and leaned forward. Like a confidant or a friend. "Just want to ask you a few questions."

The man picked up the bottle of water and drained it.

"You know, I need some water, too. If you're done, I'll bring you another bottle." The man nodded, and Cassie picked up his empty by the bottom edge and left the room.

It was an old interrogation technique. Make the perp uncomfortable by adjusting the thermostat or creating a full bladder, then suddenly they were only too anxious to talk. As an added bonus, taking the bottle was a great way to grab a set of prints, if the subject continued refusing to talk.

Noah tried again. "So, your name?"

"If I ain't under arrest, how 'bout you tell me why you dragged me in here. Otherwise I'm filing false-arrest charges." The man crossed his arms and tipped back in his chair.

"I need all four of those chair legs on the floor," Noah said.

"Or what?"

"Or I'll have to cuff you. For your own safety."

"This is some BS," the man muttered but dropped the front two legs to the floor.

Way to go, Noah. Another interrogation technique. Get a perp to comply in small ways before hitting them with the hard stuff. Nate reminded himself the man was only a person of interest, not officially a perp. Not yet anyway.

"We'd like to know why you've been following Judge Archer Bennett." Noah's voice remained neutral as Cassie returned with waters for everyone.

"Man, I don't even know who you're talking about."

After sipping some water, Cassie got that determined look. And that was the exact moment Nate understood her strategy. It was right out of the old trusty playbook—only Cassie was more subtle than most. Good cop, bad cop. Noah had gone in soft, and now Cassie...

She screwed the cap back on her bottle and in a deceptively calm voice said, "He's the man whose house you were seen outside of in Cooley. You were also spotted outside the Busy B Café, watching him through the window last night."

"You don't know what you're talking about. I ain't never been nowhere near Cooley in my whole life. Don't even know where it's at. And last I checked, it's not illegal to walk down a street outside of a diner."

"What's your purpose for being in Resolute?" Noah asked.

"None of your damn business. Got as much right to be here as you do."

Cassie twisted her lips to the side. "Hmm. All depends on what you're doing here." She took another sip of water. "So, why'd you run from us in the town square?"

And here it is. The bait and switch. Nate admired his

sister's ingenuity. She was leading the man exactly where she wanted him, like a lamb to slaughter.

"Some strange guy comes charging me, damn right I'm gonna run." The man stretched his legs out beneath the table as if getting comfortable for a casual chat. "When the two uniforms joined in…" He shrugged. "I ran faster. What can I say? It was instinct."

Cassie gave her own shrug. "I totally get it. In your situation, who wouldn't run? But just so I have this straight, you were aware that my deputy and I were chasing you?"

Her trap was set. *Now, if only…*

The man snorted. "Kinda hard to miss when you and I almost collided."

The corner of Nate's mouth turned up in a wicked grin. He glanced at Noah, who wore a similar smirk.

Apparently Sara also knew the score because she whispered, "She's got him now."

Cassie nodded at Noah. "You're under arrest for eluding law enforcement officers. You have the right to remain silent…"

While Cassie went on Mirandizing him, Noah frisked the uncooperative stalker, pulling out the contents of his pockets and setting them on the table to be cataloged as part of the booking process—a set of keys, small pocketknife, lighter, wallet and some loose change. Then he cuffed him to the bar on the table as Cassie sat and picked up her pen. "I need your name, address and date of birth."

"The hell you say. I'm not telling you anything."

Noah tsked. "Sure you want to go that route? Refusing to identify yourself when placed under arrest is another charge."

"Stubborn." Sara's face was a blank mask.

Nate wondered what she was thinking. Relieved the

nightmare was over and her life could return to normal? If so, it didn't look like it.

As the interrogation room back-and-forth continued, Nate took the opportunity to ask her again about the man. "You're positive you don't know him from anywhere? The Travis County courthouse or the DA's office? Maybe he lives in your apartment building or delivered food to you?"

Sara shook her head. "I swear, I've never met this man. If we did cross paths, I never even noticed him."

In the interview room, Cassie picked up the man's wallet and tore open the Velcro tab. "Patrick Weaver of Austin, Texas." Cassie stared at him. "Where do you know Sara Bennett from?"

The man blew out a hard breath. "I already done told you I don't know no Archer Bennett. Why would I know his grandkid?"

"Never said they were related. Interesting that you knew that."

Weaver sat straighter in his chair, concern radiating on his face for the first time since he'd been brought in. "I just guessed they were related. Same last name and all."

"Could have been his mother or his wife, and yet you knew she was his granddaughter." Cassie shrugged. "You can see why I'm having a hard time buying that you're being straight with me."

"I am, I swear. It was just a guess. Like I said—just a guess." Weaver continued to protest, but Cassie ignored him.

Over his heated arguments, she pressed her shoulder mic. "Chief Deputy Reed, please bring a tray and an inventory form for Mr. Weaver's possessions, then book him for eluding and failure to identify."

Weaver turned his head and glared at the one-way glass

with hate-filled eyes. "She's back there, isn't she? I know you are!" he screamed. "You'll be sorry!"

SARA'S ARMS QUIVERED and her forehead felt clammy as the man's cold gaze seemed to study her through the mirrored glass. When a wave of light-headedness hit her, she recognized her body's reaction as the drop after an adrenaline rush. It wasn't every day she came face-to-face with a man bent on scaring the daylights out of her—or worse, his threat of violence.

"I guess we can add criminal retaliation to his list of charges." She tried to make light of the moment even while chilled to the bone by Weaver's last words. "He's not terribly bright, is he?"

Nate continued to stare into the interview room, seemingly oblivious to her discomfort, while Adam wrapped things up with Weaver. "Clearly he has a beef with you. His rant didn't jog your memory?"

No words of comfort. No reassurance that she was safe. That hurt. Far more than she imagined.

Patrick Weaver. Who are you? She ran his name over and over in her mind, trying to pick him out from among the millions of random memories jumbled in her head. There had to be a connection. From her work as an attorney, she knew stalkers were typically highly motivated individuals. Deluded, but motivated.

"Sorry, Nate, but I have no idea why this guy has so much hostility toward me. Is it too farfetched that a total stranger has been the one trying to upend my life?" Rubbing her arms in a futile attempt to vanquish the cold tingles, she leaned against Nate for support.

Hoping for the warm comfort of his arms, Sara was left feeling deprived when he chose to leave them hanging at his sides. She pulled away from his stiff and unyielding body, blinking back hot tears of fear, anxiety, a bit of relief and a whole mess of loneliness.

"At least we know who he is," Nate said. "The department can run background checks on him now."

Wow. Talk about your sterile, professional reply. Not at all the soft words of a lover, or even the compassionate comment of a friend. Okay, so their relationship wasn't slated for the long haul, but that didn't mean it had to be completely devoid of feelings. Did it?

The door to the observation space opened, and Nate stepped even farther away as Adam leaned into the room. "While we run him through our databases, you two want to join us in the bullpen? See what we find?"

"I would," Sara replied brusquely. "What about you, Nate? Or do you consider this assignment over?" If Nate wanted to play at cold detachment, it behooved her to follow suit. She didn't suffer fools lightly, even if that fool was her. Especially then.

Nate's eyes narrowed. "I don't care how good this guy looks as your stalker—I'm not leaving your side until we have proof."

Sara nodded and followed Adam down the hall, Nate right behind her. There was a part of her that acknowledged she should appreciate that he was still in bodyguard mode even with a suspect in custody. But another part of her wasn't quite ready to deal with the case being over and Nate going back to California for good.

One issue at a time. Sitting in a chair at an empty desk, she focused on the activity in the room. Cassie and Adam had taken over bullpen computers instead of working in their offices—apparently for easier communication among the group. Sara could see a list of names on Noah's monitor as he scrolled through them.

While they ran a background check on Weaver and ran his name through criminal and fingerprint databases, Sara suddenly realized she hadn't seen her grandfather since she'd gone into the observation room. "Anyone know where Pops is?"

Noah chuckled. "Hanging out with Helen. Thick as thieves, those two. Fact is I'm pretty sure I heard Helen giggle, and that *never* happens."

Pops had been a widower for so long, Sara never considered him enjoying female companionship. She tucked the thought away for later.

Noah looked up from his monitor. "Got something. He works—or at least did—at the Travis County District Attorney's Office."

All eyes in the room swung toward Sara as her jaw dropped.

"In what capacity?" Cassie asked.

Noah's fingers flew across his keyboard. "According to this roster of employees they sent us at the start of our investigation, there's a Patrick Weaver listed as a mailroom clerk."

Nate pulled his chair closer to Sara. This time she didn't look at it as a gesture of comfort but as his eagerness to finish the job. The case against Patrick Weaver was stacking up, and Nate had just said he would leave once they had proof. "Sara? Ring any bells?"

She cursed her ability to focus intently on whatever she worked on. As an assistant DA, that had meant blocking out conversations, arguments, everything going on around her. "I think I've heard my administrative assistant address someone as Pat, but I never paid much attention. I suppose she could've been talking to the guy who delivered mail to our office."

"Maybe that's what this is all about." Adam swiveled his chair toward her. "Maybe he's been infatuated with you, and you never even knew he existed."

"Unrequited love." Noah nodded. "I've read plenty of case files about that. The person in love finally can't take being ignored anymore."

"I wasn't ignoring him." Sara's voice came out sharper than intended. "I was busy concentrating on my own work."

Cassie crossed the room and rested a hand on her friend's shoulder. "We're not saying you're to blame in any way. We're just trying to figure out a possible motive."

"What about his phone?" Nate asked. "How soon can you check its records?"

"I'll request a court order for its location data before we finish up tonight. If the data shows what I think it will, we'll have enough probable cause for a warrant to access his call and text history." She returned to her own seat and continued scanning the background check she'd been running.

"Since Sara's the judge, can't she—"

"Nope." Cassie interrupted Nate halfway through his question. "Conflict of interest. I'll have to ask the district court judge who serves Boone County."

By the time they were finished for the evening, they'd found no criminal records for Patrick Weaver. His fingerprints weren't a match for any in the databases. Cassie submitted the request for the court order, and everyone headed home to rest up and prepare for another busy day tomorrow.

Letting her grandfather sit up front with Nate, Sara relaxed in the back seat, trying to get a read on her own emotions. Relief warred with anxiety when she thought about her case. She was sure they'd caught her stalker, but the actual evidence was circumstantial.

Even if—*when*—they established his guilt, that didn't mean he'd stay locked up. As an assistant district attorney, she'd seen enough guilty people walk away on technicalities not to take conviction as a foregone conclusion. They needed more evidence because she had no intention of living the rest of her life looking over her shoulder.

Getting a read on her feelings for Nate was harder to pinpoint. Having her stalker behind bars was obviously the outcome she wanted, yet it left her relationship with Nate at a crossroads. She would no longer need a bodyguard. He would no longer need to stay in Texas.

They'd made no commitments to one another. No promises. And she realized from his behavior in the observation room that he was already putting distance between them. Physical *and* emotional distance. Not for some bodyguard code of conduct, but as a way to end things between them.

She and Nate had been sleeping together since Thanksgiving night, staying in separate rooms only since Pops had arrived. She'd known from the get-go that their relationship would be short-lived. But the thought that she'd already made love with Nate for the last time made her heart thump a sad, dull rhythm against her ribs.

Watching Resolute slide past the car window, Sara shook her head. *We didn't make love. We had sex. Love was never a factor in any of this.*

Chapter Fourteen

The next evening Sara stepped through the doorway of the Chute, reportedly the best restaurant and honky-tonk in the county. She'd heard about it when she was in town a decade ago and had wanted to check it out. She'd never made it inside then but was excited to finally see the county landmark.

As she and Pops walked ahead of Nate through the old cattle chute to the hostess stand, her head turned from side to side, taking in the busy bar on one side, pool tables and shuffleboards on the other.

"Will you look at that." Archer pointed toward the far end of the cavernous room ahead. "They have one of those mechanical bulls." He scoffed. "They've even got a line of durn fools waiting to break their necks."

Sara went up onto her toes to see the contraption she would have ridden without a second thought back in the day. Now she supposed flying through the air and landing in an undignified position wasn't the best look for the local judge.

"Howdy, Nate." The young, pretty hostess greeted him with a sparkly smile. "I hear you're quite the hometown hero."

Nate's eyebrows climbed toward his hairline. "What are you talking about, Crystal?"

She rolled her eyes. "You really think you can chase a

bad guy through the streets of Resolute—and catch him, I might add—without everyone hearing about it?"

"Gotta love small towns." Pops chuckled, and Sara joined.

Nate crossed his arms and dropped his gaze. "I'm no hero. I was just doing my job."

"And there you go, trying to be all humble on top of it." Crystal finally pulled her flirtatious gaze from Nate and turned her attention to Sara and Pops. "Howdy, ma'am, sir. Welcome to the Chute."

"Please don't call me *ma'am*. Makes me feel ancient." Sara laughed. "I'm—"

"Oh, my goodness. You're Judge Bennett. The new judge." A blush crept up Crystal's neck. "I should have recognized you straight away."

"No reason you should have. I haven't really been out and about much since I arrived." Which hopefully would change soon. She smiled, hers a lot less flirtatious than the hostess's had been toward Nate.

Pops stuck his hand out. "And I'm the new judge's grandfather." His chest puffed out in obvious pride. "No reason you should've recognized me, either." He let out a hearty laugh that put the young woman at ease.

Crystal gathered menus and napkin-wrapped silverware. "Well then, howdy, Judge Bennett and Judge Bennett's grandfather. It's a pleasure to meet you both. I'm assuming you three are part of Sheriff Reed's party?" Nate nodded. "Y'all are the first ones here. If you'll follow me, I'll get you seated."

The hostess led them through the restaurant to a round table in a secluded alcove, away from prying ears and loud customers. She placed a menu at each place setting. "I'll send your waiter over for drink orders."

As Sara started to sit, Nate took hold of her elbow and

directed her to one of the chairs against the wall. "Until further notice, we're still assuming you're in danger." He sat beside her while Pops settled in on her other side.

Her grandfather patted her knee. "I sure hope that's what this dinner is about. That they've got the right guy and can keep him locked up."

"Thanks, Pops. Me, too." She leaned her head against his shoulder for a moment before straightening, not wanting to give in to the mental exhaustion plaguing her. "Let's hope Cassie has discovered additional evidence."

Sara's curiosity about Weaver had made it hard to focus on the cases on her docket today. And then there'd been Nate. From the corner of her eye, she'd watched him standing to the side of the bench, stoically studying every face in the courtroom. He'd been civil last night and this morning. Friendly, even. But having observed the barrier he'd thrown up yesterday, she couldn't now unsee it.

A waiter, dressed in jeans and a cowboy shirt, approached the table. "Howdy, folks. My name's Justin, and I'm your server this evening. Can I get you started with drinks and an appetizer?"

"Howdy, Justin." Pops grinned at the young man. "I'll have a bourbon and branch."

"Very good, sir. And you, miss?"

Sara bit back a chuckle. Justin must've known calling a woman *miss* instead of *ma'am* made his female customers happy. "I'd like a glass of Riesling."

"Just water for now, Justin," Nate said. "Maybe something later with dinner."

"Of course, Nate. And by the way, great job yesterday. Wish I could've seen you tackle that guy." Justin turned and headed for the bar.

"My, my." Sara chuckled. "Word certainly gets around

fast in Resolute. Looks like we're having dinner with an honest-to-God hero, Pops."

"Must be why we've got this extra-special table with its own little cubbyhole."

Nate dragged his fingers through his hair. "Another reason I prefer Los Angeles. Nobody knows anybody out there."

"Ah, come on, son. Must feel pretty good to know people appreciate you so much." Pops met Nate's eyes. "And in case you didn't know, my granddaughter and I think you're a hero, too. Don't we, hon?"

Sara's smile, though genuine, tightened. "Of course we do." She unwrapped her silverware, not wanting to meet Nate's eyes. "Who wouldn't?"

Fortunately, Justin returned with their drinks. As he set a glass of ice water in front of Nate, he asked, "Sure I can't bring you something stronger?"

"No, thanks. I'm still on the clock."

"I thought the guy's locked up." Justin tucked his drink tray under his arm.

"Can't really talk about it." Nate kept his answer short. "You know, ongoing investigation."

Justin's eyes widened, and he glanced over his shoulder as if trouble was imminent before giving Nate a slow nod. "Gotcha."

Sara sipped her wine, staring blankly at her menu. Nate had just referred to dinner as still being on the clock. If she'd had any doubts that she was nothing more than a job, they were gone now. Made it difficult not to feel the fool, thinking the affection he'd shown her had been real. But nothing real could be shut off that quickly.

"Well, in case you change your mind, Sal said first round's on the house for the hero's table." Justin took off again, weaving his way through the tables in the main part of the dining room.

"Who's Sal?" Sara asked.

"The manager." Nate dropped his head back and closed his eyes. "I just hope he doesn't do something embarrassing, like make an announcement before the music and dancing starts later."

An attractive woman passing their table paused, then turned to stare at Nate. "I'm so sorry to intrude." An apologetic smile accompanied her heavy Texas accent. "But I couldn't help overhearing the waiter just now. Are you the one who arrested that strange man running through town yesterday?"

"No, ma'am." Nate managed a closed-mouth smile in return. "I'm not in law enforcement. The sheriff's department arrested him."

"But you caught him, right? That's what everyone's saying." She actually batted her lashes at him. "I just wanted to thank you for keeping our town safe. You really are a hero."

Nate studied the woman. "You were in court today, weren't you?"

"My goodness, how sweet of you to notice me, let alone remember." Her gaze floated from Nate to Sara, the woman's smile turning smug. "I was. Heard such great things about our new judge, I just had to come see her in action. A darn site more impressive than Judge Harmon." She nodded at Sara. "Well, I've taken up enough of your time. Y'all enjoy your dinner."

While the woman followed Justin's path toward the bar, Sara arched a brow at Nate. In a Southern drawl as thick as the woman's, she said, "I do declare, you have admirers wherever you go, Nathaniel Reed." She nearly gave herself a seizure trying to imitate the lash flutter.

Her comment was half teasing—but only half. And it irritated her that the other half seemed to have jealousy behind it. Sara had never dealt with the green-eyed monster in her life. There was no logic in it showing up now.

Fortunately, Nate didn't react to her words at all. He was too busy reading something on his phone after it had chimed with a text.

"Cassie says they're just leaving the justice center. They'll be here in a few minutes."

Sara leaned toward him. "Did she say anything else?"

"Nope. We'll have to wait till they get here." Nate raised his water. "Here's to good news."

"Here's to sleeping in my own bed again." Pops chuckled as he held his glass up.

Sara clinked her glass against theirs. The only wish she had about *her* bed was that Nate would share it with her one last time. Then, annoyed at herself for being so weak willed, she said, "Here's to locking Weaver up and throwing away the key."

Pops turned his attention to Nate. "What about you, son? Sara mentioned you have a big meeting coming up. When do you leave for California?"

"As soon as possible. I'd originally planned on going back right after Thanksgiving."

Her grandfather frowned. "What if my granddaughter's safety isn't a done deal by the time you're ready to go?" He smoothed his mustache. "I understand you've got a business to run. But in my book, when a man takes a job, he doesn't quit until it's finished."

"Pops…" Sara rested a hand on his arm.

Nate nodded at the older man. "I feel the same way, sir. And I'll stay here as long as I possibly can." He met Sara's eyes for a moment, then looked away. "Worst-case scenario, I'll have two of my best bodyguards from California in place here before I leave."

Sara's eyes narrowed, and she swallowed back her growing fury. Nate had no right to think he could take off and leave two strangers in her home just because he had someplace else to be.

Realizing her soft touch on her grandfather's arm had turned into a biting clench, Sara removed it and with a deep breath, focused on smoothing the napkin on her lap. She felt Pops's stare and needlessly rubbed her hands across her thighs.

Turning to Nate, Pops asked, "You saying it takes two of your men to do what you do by yourself?" He tsked. "If that's the case, sounds like maybe they're not your best men."

Nate rubbed the spot between his brows with a finger as if warding off a headache. "No, sir, that's not what I'm saying. If it does become necessary, the only reason I'd double the protection is to give Sara more peace of mind."

Peace of mind, my sweet patootie. I'd like to give you *a piece of* my *mind.*

"Hmm." Pops sounded as unimpressed as Sara was annoyed.

Nate looked at her, and out of the corner of her eye she saw his forehead crease with curiosity or concern or confusion. She wasn't sure which, and she couldn't care less.

"You okay, Sara?" Pops asked her. "You've been quieter than a possum playing dead."

"I'm fine." She forced the words out with barely moving her lips. "I'm just peachy keen and hunky dory."

"Now, don't be upset with me for grilling Nate. My main concern is your safety." Pops put his arm around Sara's shoulders for a brief side hug. "But truth be told, I'll be happy when things are back to normal, too. As much as I love spending time with you, I miss my routine at home." He chuckled. "Never thought I'd become one of those old geezers set in their ways, but here we are."

That got a snort out of Sara. "You were always set in your ways, Pops. They just changed a little with the seasons. Remember when I was there during the summers? You basically kept your routine but adapted it to include me." Sara leaned her head against his shoulder. "Now they're changing with the seasons of your life."

Her grandfather planted a light kiss on Sara's cheek. "How'd you get to be so smart?"

"I must have inherited it." She smiled as they finished their well-worn joke together. "But it obviously skipped a generation."

Her own laughter filled Sara with a warmth that lifted her mood a little. Never one to get into personal arguments in public, she'd save her quarrel with Nate for later. Maybe it would be a moot point. Maybe Weaver was their guy, Nate could head home and she wouldn't need any more bodyguards disrupting her life.

Nate better hope that turns out to be the case. Because now she wanted to be done with him. And the sooner, the better.

"SORRY WE'RE LATE."

Nate looked up to see Cassie slide into the chair next to Archer while Adam and Noah grabbed the other two empty seats. He watched them closely, looking for any hint about Weaver. Giving up, he asked, "Well?"

Cassie's mouth curled into a satisfied smile. "We got him."

Sara whispered, "Are you sure? How—" She cut herself off as Justin reappeared.

"Hey there, Cassie, Adam, Noah. How y'all doin'?"

"We'll be better after you bring us three margaritas on the rocks," Noah said. "Extra limes."

Adam glanced at Nate's glass of water. "You're not drinking?"

"Unless I'm told otherwise, I'm working." Nate shrugged.

Cassie leaned forward. "Nate, you're no longer working."

"In that case, why don't you go ahead and bring me one of those." He indicated Archer's bourbon and branch.

Justin nodded, then looked at Archer. "I'll go ahead and bring you a fresh one—" he glanced at Sara "—and another glass of wine." He stage-whispered to the newcomers, "First round is on Sal tonight."

"The court order came through." Noah's voice rose with excitement. "You won't believe what the location data showed."

Adam laid a hand on Noah's shoulder. "Let your sister tell them. The whole restaurant doesn't need to hear this."

Cassie picked up where Noah had left off. "The location data showed Weaver's phone had been in Austin until about a month ago." She met Sara's eyes. "It popped up here in Resolute the day before you arrived."

Sara's chin dropped. "He got here *before* me?"

"Probably saw that newspaper article and decided to get a head start." It was a plausible explanation, but the inferred planning involved made Nate edgy.

Cassie nodded and continued. "The phone's been in Boone County most of the time since then." She held up a finger to emphasize her next words. "Except for a trip to Cooley, Texas, for the two days right before Nate flew up to get Archer."

"That's it. You really do have him." The relief in Sara's voice was palpable.

"But wait, there's more," Noah said in a middle-of-the-night commercial announcer's voice.

"The location data gave us enough to request a warrant for the phone's calls and texts, like we'd hoped." Cassie grinned. "It was issued this morning. The phone was wiped clean, but I sent it to the forensics lab. The tech said there's a good chance they'll be able to recover everything. And those texts he sent will tie him directly to you."

"Have you found out where he'd been staying?" Nate asked.

"Not yet." Adam paused while Justin returned with their drinks, took their food order and left again. "We checked with Doc, and he thinks Weaver might have checked into his motor court for his first couple days in town. But if it *was* him, he gave a fake name—Doc's eyesight isn't the best—and the room's been turned over at least twice since then."

"So we're working outward from Resolute, checking every possibility." Cassie took a sip of her drink. "But Weaver still isn't talking."

Sara's brows pulled together. "Then you still don't know why he did it?"

Noah shook his head. "Hasn't said a word since we put him in a cell. Hasn't even asked for a lawyer."

"We're still looking at possible motives. So far, the unrequited-love idea still makes the most sense." Cassie shrugged. "If he was obsessed with you and you weren't even aware of him, it's possible in his mind he convinced himself that you were rejecting him."

"And maybe something happened without you realizing

it," Nate said. "Maybe a little thing, like he said hi to you and you didn't hear him."

Staring at nothing, Sara seemed to be rewinding her memory. "I suppose it's possible, but I don't recall anything like that happening."

"It sounds like all you've got is circumstantial evidence. Strong, but still circumstantial." Archer's expression reminded Nate of the man's long-term service in the judicial system. "At this point you can't even prove he was with his phone in Cooley."

"You're right." Cassie's tone was as grim as her expression. "But we've only had him in custody for one day. We'll get what we need to prove he's guilty." She visibly shook off her frustration and smiled at Sara. "In the meantime, we *know* he's our guy. So you don't have to live in fear anymore."

Sara returned the smile. "It sure would be nice to get on with my life."

As much as Nate had enjoyed his time in Resolute with his family, he was ready to get back to *his* life, too. Relaxing in his own place, rubbing elbows with celebrities, winning over new clients. *Trying to get over Sara* again.

When he asked about what else they'd done today on the case, Adam filled them in, from contacting the Travis County DA's office for Weaver's work history and human-resources file to trying to locate any relatives, friends or neighbors who could fill in blanks.

After their meals were served, Noah asked Nate, "So when do you blow this pop stand for Bikini Land?"

And there was the irreverent twin he knew and loved.

"As long as Sara's definitely safe—" Nate glanced at Cassie and got a reassuring nod "—either tomorrow or Friday. Depends how quickly I can get packed and book a flight."

Even as he spoke, Nate couldn't shake a vague uneasiness creeping through him. He'd like to just chalk it up to nerves about his upcoming meeting. But he wondered if it might be about leaving before he was one-hundred-percent satisfied Sara was safe, despite Cassie's assurance. He trusted his sister's confidence, and yet...

"Make it Friday," Cassie mumbled around a bite of steak, then swallowed. "We have to have a going-away dinner for you tomorrow."

"There's no need to make a big deal about this. We can consider this my dinner and—"

Cassie pointed her steak knife at him. "Nathaniel Reed, if you think you've got an ice cube's chance in hot tea of leaving town without a proper send-off, I must have dropped you on your head once too often when you were a baby."

Nate held up his hands in surrender. "Whatever you say."

"Damn straight." His sister turned to Sara. "I'll let you know the time and details tomorrow. You'll still be in town tomorrow night, Archer?"

"Of course. Maybe I can catch a ride with Nate to the airport on Friday, if our flights aren't too far apart time wise."

"I won't be able to make it," Sara said. "I promised Pops we'd spend his last night in town together, catching up."

Pops's brows angled upward in obvious surprise while her words hit Nate like a punch to his solar plexus. It seemed his attempt to put some distance between them in order to make his departure easier had backfired. He obviously hadn't handled the past couple of days well.

Amid protests from the others that Sara join them, he downed the rest of his bourbon and sighed. Just another example of him letting down people he cared about. Nate glanced at his watch and started counting the hours until he'd be back in California, where his only responsibility was his company—and there was no one to disappoint.

Chapter Fifteen

The next morning, exhausted from a sleepless night rehashing even the smallest details of the past forty-eight hours, Sara came down for breakfast to see Nate's duffel bag by the front door. At least he hadn't left for the Reed ranch, where he'd decided to stay until his flight to California tomorrow, without saying goodbye.

Low voices, as well as a dire need of caffeine, drew her to the kitchen. Pops and Nate were in the breakfast room, sitting in front of the security camera monitors.

Sara forced a cheerfulness she didn't feel into her voice. "Morning." Her mood had more to do with anxiety than insomnia, but that was her problem, not Pops's. Definitely not Nate's.

Pops turned in his chair and greeted her with a big grin. "Morning, kiddo. Nate's teaching me how this fancy security setup you've got here works."

"I'd like to show you, too, if you've got time this morning." Nate kept his attention on the screens. "It won't take long, and there's a manual in case you need to refresh your memory later."

He'd had a month to familiarize her with the cameras and alarms but had handled it all himself instead. And she'd let him. She'd allowed herself to become dependent on him for her safety instead of relying on him as an extra layer of security.

"Just let me get a cup of coffee, then I'm all yours." She kicked herself mentally as she walked into the kitchen. She *wasn't* his. She wasn't anyone's.

When she returned, Pops stood to give her his chair. "I'll let you two go over this while I make myself presentable for court."

"You plan on coming with me?" Sara could barely conceal her relief. Not that she needed anyone there. But a friendly face couldn't hurt. She'd just consider it a transition day. A bridge between having a round-the-clock bodyguard and flying completely solo.

"I wouldn't miss spending my last day in town with my favorite granddaughter if you paid me." Pops headed for the stairs.

"You do remember I'm your only granddaughter, right?" Sara called after him.

"Is that what you think? Remind me to tell you about my secret life sometime." His laughter floated back to them as he climbed to the second floor.

"He's quite the character." Nate chuckled. "Hell of a sense of humor."

"Yes, indeed." She sat in the now vacant chair and focused on Security and Safety 101. She didn't mind having the alarm system, but there was no way she would spend hours in front of these monitors, scanning the footage for a stray cat or an owl out hunting at night. Especially now, with Weaver behind bars.

Nate tapped the large, thick book. "Remember, you've got the manual if you forget any of this."

Good. Sara considered herself intelligent, but her eyes had started to glaze over by the time Nate finished the lesson.

"Well, guess I better get out of your hair." He carried his coffee mug into the kitchen and set it in the sink.

She followed him to the front door. While he picked up his duffel and computer bags, she crossed her arms over her chest. Mainly so she couldn't throw them around Nate and hug him, even if it was just a goodbye hug. "Thanks for…you know. Everything."

Nate nodded, staring at the floor as if he wanted to say something. Something important. Something that would erase the last few days and make everything between them good again. But that was just her wishing. In the end, he looked her in the eyes one last time and said, "See ya."

She was sitting at the dining room table when Pops came down a few minutes later.

He glanced at the front door. "Nate gone?"

"Yep." Like he couldn't see the bags were gone. Like he didn't know damn well Nate was gone.

Pops pulled out the chair across from her and sat. "How does that make you feel?"

She rolled her eyes. "Have you been watching TV psychiatrists lately?"

"Hey, better than TV judges."

Sara chuckled. "I don't know what I think, Pops. I thought maybe something was happening between us. But the second Weaver was arrested, it seemed like I was just a job to wrap up so he could leave town."

"There was definitely something happening between you. No doubt about it." He shrugged when she gave him a pointed look. "What can I say? Every time you two were in the same room it was hard to miss."

She planted her elbows on the table and dropped her head into her hands.

"You care a lot for him, don't you?"

Without lifting her head, Sara nodded.

"And it was obvious he cares for you."

This time she lifted her head and looked at Pops. "Could've fooled me."

"I'd guess Nate knew he had to get back to California and the way he was acting toward the end was just his way of protecting himself from getting hurt." He nodded as if approving his own idea. "Good old self-preservation."

Pops seemed to have it all figured out. But at this point, none of it really mattered. She sighed, chugged her coffee and stood. "Well, it's time to go to court."

Pops circled the table and gave her a hug. "You know you're going to be fine, don't you? However things turn out with Nate, you're tough enough to come out on top."

"Yeah, I know." But she didn't. Not really.

Chapter Sixteen

Late Friday afternoon, Nate unbuckled his seat belt as the plane taxied toward a terminal at LAX, expecting to embrace his old California attitude and lifestyle as soon as he stepped onto the jet bridge. At least, that's what he'd been telling himself he'd do for the past few hours in the air.

Despite enjoying his time at the family ranch with his siblings, much of the past year and a half had been dedicated to his father's time-consuming estate. There'd also been the grieving process for the old man, each Reed handling it in their own way.

But for the past several months, ever since the meeting with potential client Meryl Duncan had been scheduled, Nate had been champing at the bit to get back to the Golden State and once again live life on his own terms.

Unfortunately, he'd also spent his flight time telling himself to stop thinking about Sara Bennett. Not that it did any good. He hadn't been able to purge her from his thoughts since the moment he found out she was coming to Resolute.

Once the bodyguard gig started, she'd managed to upend his whole world just by being who she was. Intelligent, ethical, funny, hard-working, beautiful, kind… The list went on. And now, even though he tried not to, he missed her.

Disembarking, his steps through the terminal weren't

nearly as light as he'd hoped. Once outside, Nate hailed a cab as he turned his face up to the pleasantly temperate California sun. But instead of enjoying it as he always had, now he found it lacking, a mere imposter of the blazing orb in Texas.

He directed the cab driver to Reed & Franklin, located in the financial district southeast of downtown. Thanks to their biggest investor, none other than singing sensation Byron Cain, the company occupied the top floor of a twelve-story historical building designed in 1922.

They made the drive up I-110 in record time, quite the feat in the always dense traffic. After unloading his bags and paying the fare, Nate entered the grand old building, passing under a towering arched entryway into a cool lobby of marble and brass, then headed for the elevator.

In contrast to the building's century-old ambiance, the reception area of Reed & Franklin was urban chic with pale hardwood flooring, exposed brick and bright splashes of color accenting the modern industrial furniture. Twenty-foot floor-to-ceiling windows offered a specular view of the downtown metro area and filled the open-concept area with a flood of natural light.

"Nate! You're back." His partner, Mathew Franklin, came out of his office and headed toward him. "Should have given me a heads-up."

Parking his bags near the elevator door, he met Matt halfway for a bro hug, slapping each other on the back.

"I didn't have a lot of notice." He shrugged as he dropped down onto a sofa, stretched both arms out along the top and crossed a leg over a knee.

Matt sat opposite him in a matching chair. "You *are* back for good this time, right?"

"Ah, you missed me." Nate laughed.

"Hell yeah, I missed you. I've spent so much time in the office, I'm starting to look like a vampire. And you know how well pasty white goes over at the beach."

"Don't even try to guilt me out. It's obvious from your perma tan that you've managed to get your minimum daily dose of surfing in."

"Ha. It wasn't easy." Matt dragged his hand through his sun-bleached blond hair. "Paperwork sucks, man."

"Don't lie—Sophia handled most of the extra work while I was gone." Nate was oversimplifying the situation, and they both knew it. True, Sophia had picked up a lot of the slack while he'd been in Resolute, but Matt had done the lion's share of the heavy lifting. "Speaking of our intrepid office manager, where is she?"

"Doctor's appointment."

Nate's pulse accelerated. "Everything okay?"

"Yeah, yeah." Matt waved his hand in the air. "Just her annual check-up. She should be back by two."

Three years ago, when they'd realized managing the workload and managing the company were two different things, Nate and Matt hired Sophia Rojas as their office manager. A tall, slender woman in her midfifties with no family, she never balked at working long hours. They'd come to depend on her to the point they'd be lost without her.

For the next hour and a half, Matt updated Nate on one of their upcoming jobs—coverage during the post-season college football match-up in Pasadena. Their job would entail keeping superfans away from celebrities and former big-name players who planned to enjoy the game from the exclusive Rose Bowl Stadium suites and private boxes.

"We're fully staffed?"

Matt nodded. "Copeland and Webber will take point.

The venue exits have been mapped out, and we'll do our sweeps four hours before, then again two hours before game time. Sophia also has the timeline of activities and personal requests. So, we're all set on this one."

"Outstanding." Nate crossed the room to a mini fridge and grabbed a bottle of water. "Want one?"

"Nah, I'm good."

"Now, what about the Meryl Duncan meeting?" Nate retook his seat.

Matt grinned. "You mean our ticket to the big time?"

Reed & Franklin was in a solid financial position for a relatively small security company. Their clients paid them well, and they paid their employees well. But rent, overhead, employee benefits and all the insurance a bodyguard business needed kept them in constant search of even bigger, even higher-paying clients.

Meryl Duncan was as big as they came in Hollywood. With a word, she could make or break a company, and she wielded that power with a flippant eccentricity. She hired people on a whim and fired them with just as little thought.

Nate nodded. "Are we current on the holiday show she'll be starring in?"

"Sophia has researched all the details, prepared printouts and has them ready for us to study before we meet with her and her entourage." Matt pointed a finger at his partner. "Just remember, she specifically asked that you be at the meeting. Personally, I think she has a crush on you. Might be she's on the prowl for a new boy toy."

"*Nooo*, thank you." Nate cringed at the thought of spending personal time with the demanding diva.

Matt chuckled. "So you finally wrapped up your father's estate?"

"It's as done as it can be until Bishop finds my mother."

Nate had been friends with Matt since working bodyguard jobs together for a company in Vegas. By now they both knew pretty much everything about each other's lives.

Matt's eyes bored into his. "And Sara?"

"What about her?"

His friend's easy smile returned. "Seriously, dude. When you first told me about her, I could tell you were crushing on her hard."

"So what?" Nate gave a nonchalant shrug. "She was a favor to my sister—a job. That job is over." His gut argued with him.

"You're saying the relationship is over?"

"There was never a relationship to begin with. We both knew that going in." Even as he spoke the words, they rang hollow.

"Okay, no relationship. All over. Great." Matt slapped his knees. "On your desk is a pair of tickets to the LA Comic Con that Nashira dropped off. She said you knew about it and you better be here for it."

Nate dropped his head into his hands with a growl. "I did know. And I guess I am here." Nashira was one of the women he saw on a casual basis.

Matt's ever-widening grin proved he was clearly enjoying himself at Nate's expense. "Didn't think that was your kind of scene."

"It isn't, but I promised Nashira I'd go with her."

"Didn't think that was her scene, either."

"Nashira's scene is anywhere that she thinks she'll meet someone to further her career. I can't really blame her. Her agent's pretty worthless, but he's her brother-in-law, so she's stuck with him." Nate was already regretting his promise. "She told me some important producer will be there because he's a fan of one of the headliners. I figured as long as I had to go, I might as well try to drum up some prospective clients for us."

"Good idea." Matt gave him a thumbs-up. "I'm in awe of your always-working mentality."

"And that's why my name comes first." Nate laughed as Matt flipped him off on his way back to his office.

His laughter faded away as Nate left the building and headed home to wash off the travel dirt. To relax. To re-acclimate himself to the City of Angels, where for some reason, everything suddenly seemed slightly…off.

"Slow down, Nate. It's important that I'm seen."

Nashira Isa, an up-and-coming new face on the big screen, tugged his arm to slow his pace as they made their way through the Los Angeles Convention Center on Sunday, the final day of Comic Con.

Nate glanced at his watch. "I thought this shindig started at six." The *shindig* was an invitation-only gathering in the private suite of some big shot or another. He supposed he should pay attention to such things if he really wanted to find prospective clients, but tonight he found it hard to care.

Even at events that weren't necessarily his thing, as Matt would say, he usually enjoyed mingling. Instead, the lingering discontent that had cloaked him since his return to LA lingered. Even his craving to kick back in his own apartment had deflated after forty-eight hours alone with his thoughts.

"It *does* start at six." Nashira rolled her eyes.

"Well, it's only a few minutes till. Shouldn't we be speeding up instead of slowing down?"

Nashira tsked and shook her head but never once dropped her million-dollar smile. "Fashionably late is preferred. Really, Nate. Don't you know how to make an entrance?"

Apparently he didn't and decided the best way to get through the evening was to shut up and let Nashira take the lead.

As they continued at their slower pace, Nate took in the booths and displays devoted to comics, gaming and pop culture. They strolled past celebrities, cosplayers in full costume and normally dressed attendees.

Plenty of people were checking out Nashira, too. At five-foot-ten, she was leggy and well-rounded and showing most of it off in a miniskirt and halter top. Her long, dark hair swayed as they ambled toward the escalator that would take them to the VIP room where she hoped to meet the producer.

Normally, Nate would have taken pride in keeping company with a beautiful woman like Nashira. But tonight he felt empty, devoid of emotion as they rode up the escalator.

The women he dated were like him, looking for no-strings-attached companionship. An enjoyable evening out, an even more enjoyable night in. No promises, no regrets.

But he hadn't anticipated how sleeping with Sara, a woman he admired and respected, a woman he actually cared about, could change things. And since Nate didn't like feeling muddled, he'd left Resolute with a vow not to dwell on Sara or the time he'd spent with her. But that hadn't stopped the lingering effect she had on him.

Feelings. He snorted. More trouble than they were worth.

By the end of Sunday evening Nashira had not only failed to find her producer but had also failed to find her way into Nate's bed. And if Nashira was in a foul mood because of it, he was doubly so. She should have been the one to excise all those irritating emotions he couldn't shake. But instead, Nate had dropped her off at her place without even a goodnight kiss. He couldn't make himself want a night of meaningless sex.

THE DAY OF the Meryl Duncan meeting, Nate was driving in the morning rush-hour traffic when his cell phone rang. Noah.

Nate pushed the control for Bluetooth. "What's up?"

"Where are you?" Noah's normally light tone was absent.

"Driving. Why?"

"Pull over."

"Not a chance. I'm already late for a career make-or-break meeting. Tell me why you called now or tell me later, but I'm not pulling over." Nate wasn't usually so sharp, especially with his twin, but ever since Comic Con three days earlier, he'd maintained a sour disposition. Even Sophia had called him out for it, not that it had made a difference.

He blamed his continued moodiness on stress overload. Once the details of protecting Meryl and her considerable entourage were finalized and Reed & Franklin had a signed contract in hand, everything would go back to normal.

"Pull over, now!"

"Son of a..." Nate jerked the steering wheel hard to the right and rolled to a stop on the freeway's shoulder. "Fine. I pulled over. Now tell me what's so all-fired important."

"Sara's gone missing."

Blood rushed from Nate's head as concern ripped through his gut. "What do you mean she's missing?"

"First of all, you need to know that everyone is working twenty-four seven to find her."

"Tell me what happened." Nate's steering wheel creaked under his grip. "*Now.*"

"Sara had dinner at Cassie's place last night. They decided to have a girls' night in because Bishop was out of town and Sara's been kind of moping around since you and her grandfather left."

Nate filed that info away for later consideration. "And then?"

"Cassie said Sara left around ten and texted that she'd made it home a few minutes later. But she didn't show up for work today, and nobody's seen her since."

Nate pressed his thumb into that spot between his eyes where headaches were born.

"The bailiff called Cassie this morning." Noah took a breath. "Cassie has a spare key to the mansion, so we went over there right away. She wasn't there. No signs of a struggle or anything."

"What about her car?"

"Parked in the driveway."

Unless Sara had stopped following their security protocols, her car should have been in the garage. Which meant if someone *had* kidnapped her, it happened last night before she drove it inside or this morning right after backing it out. Then again, maybe she'd gotten lax after they'd locked up Weaver. If she'd been taken outside, the house alarm wouldn't have gone off, but...

"What about her camera feeds? They would have captured anyone on the property."

"All the cameras caught was someone wearing all black, a ski mask and sunglasses and their gloved hand as they sprayed each camera lens with black paint. We checked in the neighborhood for witnesses of that and the kidnapping, but no one lives close enough to see much."

Damn it. That sounded like the same person he'd seen on camera when Sara's tires were slashed. "Listen, I'm not trying to tell you how to do your job, but take a careful look around the garage, okay? Especially the side away from the street. Look for footprints, cigarette butts, anything."

"Bree's doing that now."

"Okay, good." Nate paused, racking his brain. "Tell Cassie to take another go at Weaver. Hard."

"She already has been, but he's still refusing to talk. So far, anyway." Noah scoffed. "Little weasel."

"Did Forensics find anything on the phone?"

"Just got it this morning. A list of phone numbers. No texts to Sara, but he was texting someone. Adam's working that angle."

"I should be there."

"There's nothing you can do that we aren't already doing. We'll have her back safe and sound before you know it."

Will you, though? Nate recognized platitudes when he heard them but decided arguing was a waste of time. "Keep me updated. Like, every half hour. Got it?"

"You bet." Noah hung up.

Passing cars on the freeway zoomed by Nate as he sat there, processing. Sara had been missing for anywhere from two to twelve hours. Weaver was still locked up. If this was connected to the stalking—and it would be one hell of a coincidence if it wasn't—that meant another player, one they knew nothing about. Thoughts of what might be happening to Sara pierced his heart like shards of broken glass.

Despite Noah's words of assurance, there was plenty he could do in Resolute. He could join the search. He could reexamine the security footage. And when Sara was found, he could be there for her.

He had spent the past month convincing her she was in danger, even if she hadn't wanted to believe it. But maybe he was the one who needed to quit lying to himself. Maybe it was time to admit his feelings for her.

He pulled up Matt's number.

"Nate. You almost here?"

"Sorry, Matt. Change of plans."

Chapter Seventeen

Sara's head lolled to the side. Trying to ignore the pounding beat of the bass drum inside her brain, she forced her eyes open. Before they slammed shut against the scorching sunlight, she caught a small crescent view of a room. A dirty, barely furnished room.

She wondered where she was but lost the thought halfway through it. Blinking away the blurriness in her vision, she realized the light was dim, not bright. Had she been blindfolded?

She went to massage her forehead with her fingers, but they weren't there. Panic gripped her—her fingers, hands, even her arms had disappeared. She twisted to peek at her shoulder, sending another blast of agony through her head. Her arms *were* there, she just couldn't feel them. They had been pulled behind her, apparently bound, completely numb. Glancing down, she noticed her ankles were tied to the chair legs.

Her tongue seemed to fill her mouth, and when she tried to swallow her throat refused to work. Alarmed she would choke to death, Sara fought against her bindings in a futile struggle. Shoving her tongue forward, it came up against a rough, nasty-tasting strip of cloth. A gag.

She forced herself to be still, taking a deep breath in

through her nose, then out. Looking around the room, she tried to get her bearings, searching for anything she could use to her advantage.

The space appeared to be a living room, maybe in an abandoned house. Trash littered the floor. Cobwebs filled the ceiling corners and hung from windows like lacy swag curtains.

Aside from two filthy upholstered chairs with ripped fabric and two sleeping bag–topped air mattresses on the floor, there was an overturned table with only three legs, a rusty metal TV tray and whatever she was sitting on.

Sara hadn't noticed the total silence surrounding her until heavy footfalls crossed the floor of another room. As the steps grew closer, Sara chose self-preservation over curiosity about her kidnapper—closing her eyes and letting her head hang forward.

Hard-soled shoes made their way toward her, grinding dirt into the hardwood floor. With each step, Sara's stomach tightened, and her mind tried to run away and hide. She cracked one eye open just enough to see Western boots pass by her.

Silence returned. Then in a flash, a hand wrapped itself in her hair and yanked her head up and back so far she thought her neck would snap.

"Nice try. You breathe differently when you're asleep."

The feminine drawl poked at Sara's memories.

Still holding Sara's hair in a painful grip, the woman circled around in front of the chair. "I won't punish you for this lie." She nodded. "It may have been nonvocal, but it was still a lie." She jerked Sara's head with each word. "However, I won't tolerate another one."

Her captor let go of Sara's hair with a shove and pulled the gag out of her mouth, leaving it to hang around her neck.

Sara recognized the woman as the one who'd approached their table in the Chute. The flirtatious one who Nate had seen in court. Blinking against the multiple drums now battling in her head, she opened her mouth, but her throat was parched, her tongue dry, her words broken. "Who... are...you?"

"Nobody you know. But you're about to." The woman pulled one of the upholstered chairs closer and plopped down on it. "Interesting how your boyfriend noticed me in court so quickly, yet I sat in a courtroom in Austin every day for a week while you prosecuted my brother and you never once looked around to see who was watching the trial, watching *you*."

"Your brother?" Sara had made it a practice to ignore the gallery of spectators when she was trying a case. Her focus had to be on the defendant and judge and jury, not weeping relatives of the victims or the defendant's furious family.

"Why don't we start with my name—see if you can figure out who he is all by yourself." She cocked a brow. "I'm Joan Dillon."

The last name was familiar, but Sara couldn't place it. As she mentally inventoried her cases, her still-fuzzy mind refused to cooperate. But the second she stopped trying, his face appeared. Not from the courtroom but from the files she and Nate had reviewed with Cassie and Adam. He'd been one of the many considered unlikely to be involved in this.

Boy, had they been wrong.

"David Dillon." Sara searched her memory. "DWI with a side order of drugs." Staring at Joan, she added, "Yeah, I can see the family resemblance now."

The woman barked a short laugh. "Well, well, well. Aren't you feisty in the face of danger."

Sara rolled her eyes. "So tell me, who's Patrick in all of this? From what I remember, you're David's only living relative."

Joan waved a hand in the air. "He's an incompetent man who's madly in love with me. A definite fly in the ointment when he was arrested, but at least he's loyal enough that he'll never give me up to the cops." She sighed, then brightened. "Obviously, the feeling's not mutual."

"Let me guess." Sara scoffed. "Because he worked in the DA's office, you arranged to meet him *after* your brother was sent to prison."

"Now don't go getting all high-and-mighty on me." Joan stood. "Seems you were doing the same thing with your bodyguard, playing kissy-face one day, then giving each other the cold shoulder the next." With a sneer, she left the room.

Even with all of Nate's security precautions, this woman knew so much about them while they knew nothing about her.

Nate. Sara took another deep breath, willing the tears to hold. She'd been missing him since before he left town, and not just because of the safety he had provided. But at this moment she'd give everything she owned to be rescued by her bodyguard. She silently cursed California and its appeal to him.

She had no idea what Joan Dillon planned to do to her, but allowing Sara to see Joan's face didn't bode well. Pops had always told her to live life without regrets. Yet right now she *definitely* had regrets. About how things had ended between her and Nate. Both times. About how she'd never get a third chance to change their future. It was agonizingly clear if Sara had a future, it wouldn't be a long one.

NATE WAITED IN the airport pickup zone, watching for Noah's vehicle. He'd called the airlines while driving to

LAX and managed to get a seat on the next nonstop flight to San Antonio. Between flight time and time-zone changes, it was already midafternoon in Resolute, and Nate had already spent too many hours imagining the worst.

He'd called his siblings several times throughout the day with the same question, always getting the same answer. Now, as he climbed into the passenger seat, he greeted his twin with a brusque hello and asked again. "Have you found her yet?"

"Not yet." Noah shook his head. "I'll catch you up on everything on the drive back."

Emotionally stretched to the breaking point, Nate buckled his seat belt and stretched out his legs. "Go ahead."

"When we got Weaver's phone info from Forensics, there was one frequently called number. Adam cross-referenced it with the list of phone numbers we created from the inmates' files."

"The ones we waded through in our first meeting?"

"Yep. He matched it to one of the numbers from those files." Noah glanced at Nate. "It belongs to a Joan Dillon. Her younger brother, David Dillon, was one of the men who threatened Sara after he was found guilty."

Nate searched his memory. "Was he the one put away for drugs?Something like that?"

"That's the one."

"So…what? He had his sister hire Weaver to harass Sara? Then who kidnapped her?" Nate pounded a fist on the dashboard. "This guy is going to pay—"

"Hold up, bro." Noah gave his brother a rap on the shoulder. "First, the vehicle is government property, so watch it." He met Nate's glare with a wink. "Second, the prison unit warden okayed a video call between Cassie and Dillon, and he didn't know anything about this."

"Why would you believe anything he said?" Nate stared at his twin. "How could Cassie be taken in like that by a criminal?"

"I know you're upset, but we'll finish this faster if you calm down and just listen." Noah gave him the side-eye. "Can you do that?"

He blew out a frustrated breath. "Yeah."

"Okay. Cassie didn't tell David what was going on at first. She just asked him if he knew where Joan was, that we had some questions about an unrelated incident." Noah flipped on his turn signal and pulled out into heavy traffic, his brows crunched into a frown. "He said his sister has psychological problems. Schizophrenia, he thinks, but isn't sure. One minute she's fine, the next she's completely out of touch with reality, ranting about conspiracy theories and such."

Nate forced himself to remain silent until Noah finished.

"Seems she's very attached to her brother and was extremely upset when he was convicted. She visited him weekly at the beginning, but when she started coming up with ridiculous ideas about breaking him out, he told her not to come anymore." Noah shrugged. "Didn't want her messing with him getting a chance at probation down the road. Apparently she told her brother about some guy she was dating who she had wrapped around her little finger. According to David, she said the guy, who she referred to as Pat, would do anything for her to make her love him. But he said Joan doesn't have the capacity to love."

Nate waited a moment to make sure Noah was done talking. "Again, why are you all so sure he's telling the truth?"

"Because when Cassie explained what had happened with Sara, Dillon seemed honestly shocked. He said if his sister was really involved in this, we needed to find her as soon as possible and get her the help she needs."

Nate looked out the side window, shaking his head in disbelief.

"*Also* because he reported all of this to the warden months ago. David informed him of Joan's bizarre ideas to break him out. Said he didn't want any trouble from her, so he wanted her removed from his approved visitors list." Noah glanced over his shoulder, changed lanes and hit the freeway on-ramp at full speed.

Frustrated with the whole situation, Nate leaned his seat back and crossed his arms.

"Dude, I understand your skepticism, but Cassie's gut feelings are almost always spot on. And I was there for the questioning, too. We all were. We stayed out of frame, but we could see Dillon's face while they talked. It sure seemed to me he was telling the truth."

"Whatever." Nate didn't have time for this. He needed to find Sara.

"You know, it doesn't matter right now if David was involved or not. He provided us with information. We can figure the rest out later."

"Can't you flip on your lights, make better time?" Nate knew he was in a bad mood and taking it out on his brother. But that was what twins were for.

"How 'bout I handle the driving and you take a look in that folder on the dash."

Nate opened the file. "What is this?"

"A printout of the texts between Weaver and David's sister. These link them together."

Nate skimmed through texts dating back to before Sara had left Austin. The two had definitely been planning something. "What about the texts sent to Sara?"

Noah shrugged. "Could have been Weaver using a burner phone, but we think it was probably Joan using a burner or a VPN."

Nate let Noah drive in peace as he read through all the text messages. Besides the connection between Patrick and Joan, one other thing was evident—this woman definitely had the poor sucker wrapped around her finger.

By the time the twins strode into the justice center, it was almost 5:00 p.m.

"About time you boys made it back." Helen caught them before they headed to Cassie's office. "You're to go directly to the observation room. Your sister's about to put the screws to that awful man you caught."

"Tsk, tsk. That's not how we talk about our prisoners, Helen." Noah enjoyed tossing back one of her admonishments.

"Y'all just do whatever you have to do to find Sara, you hear?" She was still muttering to herself as the brothers rounded the corner and moved out of earshot.

Nate led the way into the small room, where Adam and Bree were already standing. They stepped aside enough for him to squeeze in at the glass.

"You're wasting your time." Weaver leaned back in his chair. "I already told ya I got nothing to say."

"I just want to update you on what we've learned." When Weaver only shrugged, Cassie folded her arms. "We've discovered that you and Joan Dillon are in a relationship and that she's David Dillon's sister."

Weaver's eyes widened, but he remained silent.

"Now, Patrick, here's the thing. We already have evidence tying you to the harassment and stalking of Judge Sara Bennett." Cassie leaned forward. "And now we're going to have to charge you with her kidnapping."

"The hell you say!" Weaver jumped up, but his hands, cuffed to the table, kept him right where he was. "I got nothing to do with any kidnapping."

"But you knew Joan was planning on taking the judge. To what end? Hurting her? Killing her for proving her brother was guilty and helping to send him to prison?"

Nate understood why Cassie had asked that last question, but to hear his deepest fear voiced out loud made his head spin. He took a deep breath and refocused.

"I'm not saying another word."

"Have it your way. But Joan *did* kidnap the judge. And you'll be charged as an accomplice in anything she's done or is about to do." Cassie stood. "I was hoping you'd cooperate with us in return for reduced charges. Especially since Joan knows you're in jail and has hung you out to dry." She walked toward the door.

"Wait a minute." Weaver licked his lips. "Honest, I didn't know she planned on kidnapping the lady. All Joan told me was she wanted to scare her on account of her brother."

Cassie returned to the table and sat. "Where is Joan?"

He opened, then closed his mouth, his head tilted. "What'd you mean you could get my charges reduced?"

"Just that. I'll go the district attorney and ask that you not be charged with kidnapping." Cassie gave him a moment, then asked again, "Where is Joan staying?"

"Well, I don't know for sure. She was bouncing all over the place looking at houses, and—"

Cassie sighed and stood. "Good luck in prison, Patrick."

She hadn't even made it one step. "It's an abandoned house out in the country," Weaver said, his voice trembling. "I don't know how to get to it. I was only there once, and Joan drove. It…it was white. Some of the windows were boarded up. There weren't any other houses close by."

"If you were only there once, where were you staying the rest of the time?" Cassie looked up from the notes she'd been scribbling.

"Joan got us a room in some lousy motel outside of town. We only moved to the house the day before y'all caught me."

"Which direction did you go to get to the house?"

"Well, our motel was west of town. Last thing I remember as a landmark was a big school, then we turned right, so we had to be going south." He looked up to the left, rubbing his chin. "Yeah, southeast of town."

Without glancing up, Cassie asked, "What's she driving?"

"A van. An old blue one, with patches of body filler. Joan's a lousy driver." When Cassie glared at him, he shrugged. "I don't know the make or model. All I know is it's ugly."

Cassie left the interview room to the sound of Weaver calling after her, "Hey, what about my deal? You gonna talk to the DA? We made a deal, right?"

Coming in to join the others, Cassie broke her glare with a wink at Nate. "Got 'em."

"A white house, southeast of town." Nate cursed under his breath. "Seventy-five percent of the houses in Boone County must be white."

"Adam's already sectioned a map into areas for each of us to search. If anyone finds a possible location, you radio for backup. Understand?" Cassie looked at each person in the room. "Here's yours." She handed Nate a copy of the map with his area outlined in yellow.

He headed for the door, but Cassie called him back.

"Here's a picture of Joan Dillon. Might help if you know who you're looking for."

Nate grabbed the photo, glanced at it and froze.

"What's wrong, bro?" Noah asked.

"Nothing." He didn't have the time to explain where he'd seen the woman before. And it didn't matter. All that mattered was finding Sara before it was too late.

AS DUSK FELL, Nate drove south from town with the map app open on a tablet he'd borrowed from one of the deputies. He scanned it at stop signs, searching for houses without close neighbors. Even with that, he had to check out each house, searching for boarded-up windows and an old blue van.

Since he'd left his personal truck at the ranch when he flew to LA, Cassie had also loaned him an official sheriff's department vehicle, complete with a spotlight. He could use it when it got too dark to see, but it would also announce his presence. Maybe he'd be able to get by with the light from the almost full moon.

With both eyes peeled for the house and van and one ear listening to the occasional radio chatter between the other searchers, Nate's mind returned to Sara. If he was honest with himself, it had never left her.

He kicked himself mentally for skipping town while still uneasy about Sara's safety. But after being assured the right guy was locked up, Nate had chalked up his apprehension to the way things were being left between him and Sara.

"I might have something." Noah's voice came through the radio. After a moment of silence, he added, "Never mind. The house is light yellow."

Nate resumed the grid he was driving in his sector, about two miles south of town. The houses, farther apart now, sat back from the road. A lot of property between them seemed to be dedicated to crops. Some had barns. He agonized over the slower pace as darkness continued to fall, making it harder to make out details.

As he idled near a farmhouse surrounded by fallow land,

the clouds pulled apart and the moon lit up the scene. Most of the paint had peeled off the structure, but what remained was white.

Rolling forward, Nate looked for signs of life. No movement. No vehicles. He continued down the street, but a glint in his side mirror caught his eye. It might have been nothing, but his gut told him to go back.

He turned at the next cross street and parked, making sure the vehicle remained out of sight from the house.

With no fences around the property, Nate made his way through the dormant field behind the house. He ran from tree to tree, changing his tune now and begging the clouds to block the bright moonlight so he wouldn't be seen coming.

A dilapidated barn sat behind the house. He sprinted inside and pressed himself against the doorframe, then peeked around it. The glint he'd seen was a reflection off a vehicle. A blue van, splotched with gray patches, practically touching the back door.

Relief from finding the house was short-lived as he wondered if he'd found it *in time.*

He crept around the two-story house, making note of the windows—some boarded up, some missing, a few with broken or even intact panes of glass. Although the front door was clear, the van blocked access to the back door. When he tried to push through a holly bush to stand next to a window, its prickly leaves hooked into his jeans and scratched his hands, but he finally managed to peek through the filthy glass.

His shoulders sagged with relief. Luck must've been on his side, as the window he chose showed him Sara. She was sitting in a chair in the middle of the room, her ankles bound to the wooden legs, her arms cuffed behind her. Instead of fear or defeat distorting her features, she held her head high in defiance as she stared down the woman he now knew as Joan Dillon.

Nate wished he could call for backup, but he didn't have a shoulder mic and there wasn't time to go back and use the vehicle's radio. He pushed his ear closer to the thin glass.

"What did you expect? That I could just walk into a prison and demand an inmate be let go?" Sara scoffed.

"You put him in there, you can get him out." Joan walked into view. "Call the judge who was at my brother's trial and tell him you screwed up."

"It doesn't work that way."

"It should be even easier since you're a judge now, too. Tell him you'll owe him one."

Sara looked at the other woman as if she'd just landed from another planet. "Look, if you want your brother to get out, you should go back to Austin and hire a lawyer to file an appeal. You need to prove he's innocent before they'll let him go. And there's nothing I—or anyone else, for that matter—can do to circumvent the judicial process."

"So what you're telling me is you're no use to me." Joan crossed the room and picked up something from a table. "Is that right?" She sauntered back and stopped, facing Sara. Dim light from a camping lantern flickered off the shiny blade of a large knife in her hand.

Nate didn't wait to see Sara's reaction. Determined to draw Joan's attention from Sara, he plowed through the thorny bushes and kicked in the front door.

Joan spun toward him and raised the knife in an overhead grasp. "Ah, it's the judge's boyfriend, come to save the day."

Holding his hands up, Nate showed her he had no weapon. "Nobody needs to get hurt here." He looked past

Joan to Sara and saw a tiny smile of relief curling the corner of her mouth.

Joan followed his gaze, an ugly sneer transforming her face. "Stop talking to each other with your eyes. I know what you're trying to do. You think I can't tell what you're saying?"

If he could have told Sara anything with his eyes, it would have been how much he loved her, how scared he was to lose her. But he doubted his message would make it past a woman with a large knife amid a break from reality.

During her rant, Nate started moving slowly, trying to circle around her and get closer to Sara. Suddenly, Joan stopped speaking. She cocked her head, her gaze ping-ponging between Sara and him.

"Where do you think you're going?" She took a step toward Nate.

"Just checking to make sure Sara's all right." He shrugged and took a deep breath, knowing what he was about to say could make things better—or much worse. "David wants to know she's safe."

"Why would my brother want that? You don't even know my brother." She took another step.

"Yeah, I do. He's worried about *you*, too. He doesn't want you to get hurt, either." Nate stopped moving, worried if he got too close to Sara, she'd be within Joan's reach. "And I gotta say, he sounded pretty upset with you. Said if you hurt the judge, they're going to lock him up in solitary and he'll never get out."

"You weren't supposed to tell him!" she yelled. "This was going to be a surprise!" With a demonic shriek, she came at Nate with the knife.

Ducking to the side, he dodged the knife and grabbed her arms. They crashed into an armchair and flipped it backward, the knife flying from Joan's grasp. She twisted beneath Nate, trying to squirm out from under him, but he wasn't about to let her get to the knife. Wrapping his arms around her, he held her back to the floor, their legs still tangled together on the back of the chair. He just needed to get a grip on her arms and—

"Damn it!" The witch had chomped down on his bicep and wouldn't let go.

Nate gritted his teeth against the sound of tearing flesh, the scent of blood and its warmth as it flowed past his elbow. With his other arm, he grabbed her hair and tried to pull her head away from him.

Out of his clutch now, Joan seized the opportunity and scrambled out from beneath him. Nate grabbed for her ankle. Kicking back with her other foot, she rammed her boot heel into his face.

Dazed, Nate kept moving despite the pain. Despite the blood dripping from his fingers. Despite the grisly hole in his arm. He rose and went after the deranged woman as if Sara's life depended on it. Because it did.

Joan wrapped her fingers around the knife handle and struggled to her feet. Swinging the blade wildly toward Nate, she lost her grip on the knife, and it flew from her hand. Her momentum carried her forward at an odd angle, and she lost her balance, falling sideways. Clutching the small table to break her fall, she pulled it down with her as she went, along with the camping lantern.

Oil spilled across the wooden floor and ignited.

Grabbing the knife, Nate rushed to Sara and cut her bindings. "Are you all right?"

Sara nodded. "Just need to get the blood flowing again." She shook her arms out and cautiously tried to stand. Nate scooped her up into his arms and dashed outside to safety.

But once Sara was free from danger, he ran back inside to save Joan.

The house was a tinderbox of dry and rotted lumber, and the blaze had already climbed the walls to the ceiling. Nate tried to reach Joan, but with each attempt he was driven back by heat and flames. Choking on smoke, unable to see anything, he gave up and made his way back to the front door.

Almost there, an ear-splitting crack sounded, and Nate looked up just as the second floor crashed down on top of him.

Chapter Eighteen

The rhythmic beeps of hospital machines monitoring Nate's vital signs almost lulled Sara to sleep. She fought the urge, watching a muted home-improvement show on the small television in the ICU room. The beeps were good signs. Signs that he was breathing, his heart was beating, he was alive.

Sara's tired gaze drifted to Nate. During the twelve hours since she'd pulled him from the burning house, the bruise on his face had started to darken. Almost like a tie-dyed superhero's mask. Which was what he was to her.

Cassie, Adam and Noah had filled her in on everything that had happened after she'd been kidnapped. The search, Weaver's information, Nate's return to Resolute the minute he'd learned she was missing. She'd even overheard Noah tell Cassie that Nate had been on the plane to Texas while his important meeting had started without him.

The guilt she felt for being the reason he'd missed that meeting was only a fraction of the amount of love she felt for him. She'd tried not to admit it to herself, and she would probably never tell him. She'd already messed up his life enough.

After pulling her chair closer to his bedside she touched his cheek, the stubble stinging her fingertips. She jerked her fingers back when he stirred, his eyes drifted open and a small smile curled his dry, chapped lips.

"Hey, you." Sara's voice threatened to crack as her heart eased at the sight of Nate awake for the first time.

He croaked out what sounded like *Hey* in return, then reached for his throat. Sara picked up the cup of ice chips that the nurses had replenished each time they'd melted and held it for him until a few slipped into his mouth.

"That should help a little." She set the cup on the tray table, then brushed a lock of stray hair from his forehead.

Nate's eyes followed the movement, the lines between his brows deepening. "What happened?" he asked, his voice hoarse as he motioned toward her gauze-wrapped hands and arms.

"This?" She raised her arm and glanced at it. "This is nothing. Just a few blisters from the fire. No big deal."

He seemed to study her then, starting from the top. Her singed hair, the red streak across one cheek, the bandages on her arms and hands. "How did you get burned?"

"Well, I wasn't going to leave you in that house to die." She kicked up one side of her mouth in a smile. "Didn't seem right after you'd just finished saving me."

"The ceiling collapsed." Nate cocked his head. "You pulled me out?"

"Don't sound so surprised." She cleared her throat of tears, striving for levity. "I'm not as wimpy as you thought I was when you were my bodyguard." Sara raised one brow. "You just refused to let me be the strong, awesome woman I am."

He started to laugh, then stopped. "Ouch."

Sara's eyes widened, and she half stood from her chair. "Are you all right? What hurts?"

"Seriously?" Nate snorted. "Better to ask me what doesn't."

His small smile calmed her. "But mainly my shoulder. And my face."

"If *you* think your face hurts you, you should see it from this side. It's painful." Sara laughed when his eyes widened in indignation. "Sorry—I couldn't pass up an opportunity like that."

"You've got a wicked sense of humor." Nate chuckled. "Looks like there's a lot more for me to learn about you."

Sara gave him an impish grin. "More than you can imagine."

"So what are all these tubes they've got stuck in me?" He eyed the machines and the drip bags hanging next to his bed.

"I'm not sure, but I know the most important one is pumping antibiotics into you. Apparently human bites are even more dangerous than they are painful. All kinds of nasty bacteria and stuff." Sara's lip curled in disgust. "The nurse said you'll be on this first round for at least another day, then they'll do surgery to repair the ripped muscle in your shoulder. That woman must have had extremely strong jaws."

"Speaking of Joan Dillon, they find her body?"

Sara nodded. "They haven't done an autopsy yet, not that there's much left for one. But the medical examiner told Cassie the spilled oil probably soaked into Joan's clothes right away, based on how I explained what happened." She looked down at her hand and fiddled with a loose string from the gauze. "You went back in to save her, didn't you?"

Nate was quiet for a while. Long enough that Sara wondered if he'd answer. Finally, his eyes focused on the side of the bed opposite where she sat, he spoke. "If there was any chance she was alive, I had to try."

Learning that he wouldn't let anyone, no matter how horrible they might be, die if he could prevent it, reinforced her opinion of him. "You're a good man, Nate. I admire your integrity."

"Just the way I was raised, I guess. I didn't always get along with my dad, but I learned a lot from him. He lived by his principles and ethics." He half shrugged, the movement of even his good shoulder making him wince. "I bet after all this, you can't wait to leave Resolute in your rearview mirror on your way back to Austin. Think you'll finish out Harmon's term or head out as soon as possible?"

Taken aback by his abrupt change of subject, Sara said, "I have no intention of skipping out on a commitment." It was her turn to get quiet, to put a voice to all the things she'd been considering since the abandoned house, when she hadn't known if she'd have a tomorrow. "Besides, all of this started when I lived in Austin and…" She smoothed the small section of blanket in front of her. "I've been doing a lot of thinking. I'm not so sure I want to go back."

Nate's forehead furrowed. "Where will you go, then?"

"Nowhere." At his look of confusion, she continued. "I'm going to stay right here in Resolute. When Harmon's term is up, I'll run and hope to win."

Nate closed his eyes for a long moment, then opened them again, catching hers. "And leave your luxury-condo living behind? The big city and all its attractions? I thought you wanted that top judge job in Travis County?"

Sara didn't flinch, in spite of the current of emotion she felt as they gazed into each other's eyes. "Somewhere along the way, I confused what I thought I *should* want for what I actually wanted," she admitted.

"I don't understand." Nate pressed the remote to raise the head of his hospital bed higher.

"In my mind, becoming a district judge in Travis County

would be a way to be closer to Pops. More like him—because he was a district judge. And Travis County because it's where I was living and it wasn't all that far from him."

"So what's changed?"

"I have. My life has." Sara sighed, suddenly nervous. She hadn't planned on opening up about this to Nate. "I think I was always equating career with family. Aside from Pops, what I've never had, what I've always wanted is family. Family, friends and a simple life. And I have all that now. Here in Resolute." She laid her hand on his arm. "I'm treated like I'm one of the family when I'm at the ranch. I've met more people in the past month that I meet in a year in Austin, unless you count criminals," she said, laughing. "Between Cassie, Rachel, Bree, Marge, I'm well on my way to having lots of friends for the first time in my life. Even Helen tries to mother me, but in a good way."

Nate shifted in the bed, groaning when his sore shoulder moved. "Let me get this straight. You're planning on living in Resolute for the foreseeable future, continuing as the Boone County judge—"

"*If* the people elect me."

"Yeah, well, I have no doubt about that." He narrowed his eyes. "You honestly don't think you're going to get bored in our little Podunk town? Where you have to drive to Victoria to buy your fancy kitchen gadgets and coffees and such?"

"Oh, Nate. Living in California, I'm sure you know about online shopping and delivery. And besides, once I move all my stuff down here, there shouldn't be much else I'll need." Sobering, she added, "I never really loved living in Austin. I tried to. I convinced myself I did. But I never felt like I belonged. My entire existence revolved around work. I'm learning there's more to life than that."

Nate nodded. "I know what you mean."

He seemed thoughtful, and Sara worried that she'd over-stayed her visit. "I'm sorry—you must be exhausted. And it's probably time for more pain meds." She stood from the bed. "Thank you for saving my life."

He glanced up at her with a cryptic expression on his face. "Thanks for saving mine."

MOVEMENT IN NATE'S peripheral vision had him turning his head toward his hospital-room door. Three balloons, shaped like bananas, bobbed in midair.

"Come on in, Noah."

The door opened wider, and the balloons bounced into the room, followed by his twin.

"Recovered from your surgery?" Noah pulled a chair over to the bed, sat and let go of the balloons. Which, for some weird reason, stayed right next to him instead of float-ing up to the ceiling.

"I don't think so. They said I can go home Monday. What's today?"

"Whoa, you must be on some good drugs." Noah snick-ered. "Today's Saturday. You had your surgery yesterday. You know, Friday."

"Why are those balloons just sitting there?"

"They're not. They're standing." Noah pulled the bal-loons higher and showed Nate the cardboard feet connected to each string. "See?" He laughed.

Nate started to shake his head but stopped. Everything hurt. "Why bananas?"

"They were on sale." He gave one of the banana balloons a little push, and it waddled away. "Hours of amusement for the bedridden." Noah took a long look at his brother. "Seriously, how're you feeling?"

"Probably better than I look." He managed a small grin.

"Well, that's a good thing. 'Cause, boy howdy, you look like you were pulled through a knothole backward."

They laughed together, but when Nate winced, Noah sobered. "Sorry. I should have waited until you're better before I said anything funny. Even if it *is* true." He cleared his throat. "But at least now I can prove I'm the handsome one—instead of just claiming to be."

"Well, you better make the most of it while it lasts. Soon as this bruise drifts south of my chin and everything else heals up, you'll be back to runner-up Twin of the Year."

"I guess coming close to death like you did has an effect, huh?" Noah batted at one of the balloons.

Nate dragged his good hand through his hair. "It's not that."

"Then what?"

"Sara came to see me a few days ago." He ran his fingers across his blanket, remembering how she'd done the same thing when she was there. "She said she's not going back to Austin. Plans on staying right here in Resolute."

Noah folded his hands and rested his chin on his two forefingers. "Is this a good thing? Or a not-so-good thing?"

Nate shrugged. "Ow. I've got to stop doing that, damn it."

"Stop avoiding the question, bro."

"I guess it's a good thing for her, since it seems to be what she wants. It just surprised me. She had her life plan set in stone, and all of a sudden she changed it."

"Sometimes people change and their plans change with them. I think it's great that Sara realized she has a new definition of happiness and she's going for it." Noah kept eye contact with his brother. "What about you?"

"Me?" Nate frowned.

"Yeah. You." He raised his brows. "You ever think about changing your life plan?"

Nate shook his head. "No. At least not intentionally. But this last time I was in LA, things felt different. Off."

"How so?"

"I'm not sure." He blew out breath, searching for a way to explain it. "It was like the Golden State lost its shine. But now I'm wondering if it ever really had it." Nate scoffed. "You know what's weird? I never planned on going to California in the first place. I just wanted to get as far away from Dad as possible while I figured out how to make my own way." He felt foolish admitting this to Noah, but at the same time it was a relief. "I never really felt like I fit in out there. Even after living there all these years, I still felt like an imposter. A country bumpkin who put on an expensive suit to mingle with the beautiful people."

"Then why go back?"

This was a different Noah than Nate was used to. Asking hard, probing questions instead of the constant jokes.

Noah waved his hand. "Never mind. Let me ask you another question—why haven't you ever come back to Resolute?"

Nate didn't have to think long. "Because I never had anything to come back to. I mean, besides you guys, and you all have your own law enforcement thing going. I used to feel like the odd man out here, too."

"You feel that way this past year, year and a half?" Noah wasn't going to let up.

"No," Nate admitted.

"But still don't have anything to come back to?" His twin stretched his long legs out and crossed one boot over the other. "Nobody?"

Nate chewed on his lower lip for a while, an image of

Sara in his mind. He'd come back in time to save her life, but had he come back in time to win her heart? "Maybe."

"Was that so hard?" Noah laughed. "You both made the same decision. Sara's just smarter and braver than you, so she was willing to make it first."

"Look, Noah, I don't know if I have an snowball's chance in hell with Sara—"

"Trust me, you do. I know it, everyone knows it." He picked up one of the banana balloons and danced it around the room, singing, "My bro's finally in love."

"I KNOW, MATT. Yeah, I know."

Nate's first day home from the hospital wasn't going well. Pain pulsed in his shoulder. Even if it hadn't, that arm was in a sling, so he was basically one-handed. The bruise on his face had followed gravity's pull, so his mouth and chin were light purple while his eyes and nose had turned putrid shades of yellow and green. And he was talking to Matt for the first time since skipping out on the Meryl Duncan meeting.

"I'm sorry," he said. "I don't know what else to say."

"How soon will you be back on the West Coast?" Matt's usual levity had levitated up and out of the earth's atmosphere.

Nate propped his phone between his good shoulder and his ear as he lay on the couch. He was recuperating at the ranch with his siblings waiting on him, and he'd insisted on spending days in the living room so they wouldn't have to constantly run up and down stairs. "I'm not sure. They did surgery on my shoulder Friday, and this thing hurts like a son of a—"

"Sorry your shoulder hurts, Nate. But I can't keep things running on my own anymore."

An unfamiliar tone in his partner's voice alerted Nate that something was up, and he blew out his own frustrated breath. "We need to talk, Matt."

"Dude." Matt snorted. "I've heard that from enough women over the years to know exactly what it means."

"I'm sorry, but I've decided I want to move back to Texas." Like the release from a pressure valve, his stress dissipated in an instant.

"Wow. Well, this makes my news easier to break." He coughed out a nervous laugh. "Remember when I said I thought Meryl had a crush on you? Well, was I ever wrong."

"No. Don't tell me…"

"Yep. Meet Meryl Duncan's new bodyguard boy toy."

All Nate could think to say was "So she signed the contract?"

"Yes, she did. But, uh, she wants me to take point on the holiday celebration."

"That's fine. You were already pretty much in charge anyway." Nate couldn't understand why his partner sounded shaky.

Matt took a breath. "The thing is, starting with New Year's Eve, she wants me as her full-time bodyguard."

"Wow." Again, total loss for words.

"But she wants me as a direct hire instead of through the company. She said she'll use Reed & Franklin for big events and galas, but basically, she's buying me from you." Matt laughed. "But you're gonna love the price."

Nate wasn't sure if it was his meds or lack of sleep or nerve damage from the kick to his face, but his forehead suddenly felt numb. "Good for you. If this is what you want to do, go for it." He really was happy for his friend. He just didn't know how long Matt would survive in the clutches of Meryl.

Matt's voice smiled over the phone. "I'm happy for you, too. Does this have anything to do with Sara?"

"It might. Too soon to say."

"I hope it works out for you. It was pretty easy to tell when you came back this last time that you left part of yourself behind in Texas."

Apparently Noah was right—*everyone* had known before Nate realized it himself.

Matt broke into his thoughts. "But what about the company? If you're staying in Texas—"

"Don't worry about it." Nate's mind was racing, but at a snail's pace. "Can you and Sophia handle the event without my help?"

"Absolutely. Everything's planned out and ready to go. And I can deal with any other jobs we've got through the end of the year."

"Perfect. How 'bout you and I meet up after the holidays, figure the rest of it out." Nate was relieved, a little sad, but mostly he considered this another sign that he was making the right decision.

After ending the call, Nate almost didn't take his pill. But the nurse had stressed he should stay ahead of the pain, so he reached for the bottle just as Sara walked in from the kitchen. Cassie had insisted she stay in the guest room until her burns were healed.

"Here, let me get that for you." She hurried to the coffee table and picked up the bottle before remembering her fingers were too sore to open it. She handed it back to him. "We're quite the pair, aren't we? One hand between the two of us."

Nate chuckled. "At least we're on the mend." He washed his pill down.

Cassie had left a stack of blankets and pillows on the

leather armchair near the couch, so Nate turned onto his side and offered the empty space to Sara.

She perched on the very edge, stiff and proper. "I don't want to hurt your arm."

"Relax. My arm is fine." He shifted more against the couch back. "There's plenty of room."

She resettled herself, now leaning against his thighs. "Sorry, but I was in the kitchen and couldn't help but overhear your phone call." She met his eyes. "Did I hear right? You've decided to stay in Texas?"

Nate nodded. "Yes. I think it's time."

"Your family will be happy to hear that." She pressed the edge of the quilt, just as she had the blanket in the hospital.

"What about you?"

Sara swallowed and looked away. "Me, too." She cleared her throat and forced out a small laugh. "It's just too bad you were such a thorough hero, you know? Now I don't need a bodyguard."

"How about a boyfriend?"

She blinked her wide, blue eyes. "I—"

"I love you, Sara. And I'm sorry as hell it took me so long to realize it. And even longer to admit it." He chuckled. "Cassie did say she dropped me on my head when I was little."

"They do say third time's the charm." Sara laughed as tears shimmered in her eyes. "And the thing is, I fell in love with you along the way, too." A small frown fought with her smile. "But are you sure you'll be satisfied in Resolute? You only ever wanted to get away from here."

"I never had a reason to stay before." He reached up and ran his hand through her new pixie haircut, necessary after the fire. It suited her, framing her face and showing off those big pale blue eyes. "Now I have the best reason of all."

Epilogue

Christmas, one year later

"Just a minute," Sara called out as she took one last look around her home, *their* home, before answering the doorbell. She'd had her first full-on family Christmas last year at the Reeds. But this year she'd asked if anyone minded her hosting the holiday, and the approval had been unanimous.

Nate had moved into the judge's mansion with her after they'd recuperated from their injuries almost a year ago, and life was everything she'd hoped it could be.

The bell rang again, and she rushed to open the door.

"Merry Christmas." Noah came in, carrying a pile of gifts. "Anyplace in particular for these?"

She pointed to the front living room. "Under the tree." Taking one of Bree's side dishes, Sara led her to the kitchen.

"Oh my gosh." Setting down her crudité platter, Bree inhaled until Sara worried she'd pass out. "It smells amazing in here."

"Thanks." Sara beamed. "I've never been much of a cook, but a judge's hours aren't quite as horrendous as an assistant DA's." She shrugged. "I've been having fun learning new things."

Bree glanced at the row of small pots on the window-sill, each sporting a different limp or dead herb. "Uh-huh."

Sara laughed. "Hopefully my cooking skills are better than my black thumb."

The doorbell rang again.

"I've got it!" Nate bellowed.

She returned to the foyer to find it filled. Nate took coats and jackets while she directed Adam and Rachel's mom, Martina, to the kitchen with their dinner contributions. Meanwhile, Rachel, approaching her due date with twins, herded Brad and Daisy into the front room.

The front door swung open again, and Marge and Doc pushed into the crowd, each carrying four boxed pies from the Busy B Café.

"Ha! You should've seen the look on Cassie's face when I told her *I* was bringing the pies." Marge barked out a laugh. "Don't worry, hon. I'll find the kitchen on my own. I've got a nose for it." Chuckling, she headed down the hall with Doc at her heels.

"The house is beautiful, Sara." Martina gave her a hug. "I hope it's okay that I just set everything on the counter."

"Thank you. And of course it's okay." She leaned in closer and asked in a low voice, "How's Rachel? She looks… uncomfortable." They both turned to watch Martina's daughter waddle over to the sofa near the tree.

Martina tsked. "That would be an understatement. But she's excited that it's two more girls because Daisy's been much easier to handle than Brad. I just don't think she re-alizes she's comparing a two-year-old girl to a six-year-old boy." She gave Sara a wink. "Doesn't matter—boys or girls, she's gonna have her hands full."

Sara turned and bumped into Adam.

"Merry Christmas. And well done in the kitchen." He gave her a bear hug.

"Thanks for all the secret lessons," she whispered.

Just like Bree, Adam inhaled deeply. "I think the student may be surpassing the master."

"Trust me," Sara said, glancing down at the small nicks on two of her fingers from today's kitchen activities, "that will never happen."

Adam joined the throng in the living room, and Daisy came toward him with her arms out. "Daddy!"

As he swung her up in his arms, Brad shot past him like a greased pig at the county fair, skidding to a stop in front of Sara. "Did you know my mom's having *two* more babies?" Sara nodded, and Brad added, "Two more *girls*." He rolled his eyes, then took off running.

A blast of cold air hit Sara as Helen and Cassie came in.

"Here." Cassie handed Sara two packages of store-bought dinner rolls. "Instructions say you just have to warm 'em up in the oven." She yanked her jacket off and handed it to Nate as he walked past. "Best I could do since Marge stole my usual contribution."

"These will be great. I forgot all about rolls." Sara hugged her best friend. "Merry Christmas."

"Merry Christmas. Where's the wine?"

"You know where it is." She chuckled. "Help yourself."

Cassie turned when she was halfway down the hall. "Want me to bring you a glass?"

"We're eating in a few minutes. I'll have some then."

Nate came up behind her and snaked his arm around her waist. "I think everyone's here." Nuzzling her neck, he mumbled, "How soon can we get rid of them?"

Laughing, Sara swatted his arm. "All right, everyone,"

she said, raising her voice over the conversations. "We're going to have dinner first, then we'll open presents."

"Where's Archer?" Helen attempted to sound casual, but Sara had to bite her lip to keep from smiling. She and the Reeds had known for quite a while now that her grandfather and Helen had been enjoying each other's company. Pops said he visited often to see Sara, and while that might've been true, she knew that his recent look into local real estate probably had more to do with his new ladylove.

"He's setting up extra seating in the breakfast room."

Helen made a noncommittal sound and hurried down the hall.

Sara winked at Nate, then headed toward the kitchen.

"Here's a warm dish." Cassie stopped at the sideboard, looking around. "Is there an extra trivet anywhere?"

Bree moved one over. "Here you go. How many more do we need?"

"Beats me. I'm just bringing out what they hand me." Cassie returned to the kitchen.

Sara scooped stuffing from the turkey, Noah poured wine and everyone else except the kids and the older generation carried dishes of food into the dining room. When Adam handed Nate the carving knife, there was a brief look of confusion on Nate's face.

"Hey, man. Your house, your bird." Adam dropped into a chair, leaning back with a grin. "I'm just here to eat."

"Actually, it's Sara's house." Cassie pulled out a chair. "I mean, it *could* be Nate's house if he made an honest woman out of my best friend."

Nate's siblings all chuckled over the joke they'd kept up ever since Nate moved in last year.

Nate rolled his eyes and offered Sara the knife. "Would you like the honors?"

Sara raised both hands with a laugh. "Oh, no. I'm taking a page out of Adam's book." She quickly sat. "I'm just here to eat." Sara threw Cassie a look. "And as a judge of this here county, I take exception to you implying I am any less honest of a woman simply because I don't have a ring on my finger." She knew everyone was waiting for the last Reed to settle down—legally. But as Sara felt more loved and more secure in that love than she had in her entire life by simply having Nate by her side, she had no complaints about her bare ring finger.

"You do know how to carve a bird, don't you, son?" Pops, cheeky grin in place, raised an eyebrow at Nate.

Sara fought sudden tears when Pops gave her a wink. The Christmases they'd had together when she was a kid had been simple with just the two of them but happy.

Now, seeing the joy on his face and the glint in his eye, she knew she hadn't been the only one yearning for more. More family. More holiday spirit. More noise.

And they finally had it.

Nate squared up to the turkey like a man about to do battle. "Yes, sir."

And while the bird might have gotten a tad more chopped than carved, it was just as delicious.

HOURS LATER AND guests gone, Sara found Nate sitting on one of the sofas in the living room. He was gazing at the brightly lit Christmas tree as carols played softly in the background.

Sinking into the spot next to him, Sara leaned against him, exhausted, stuffed and spotting bits of ribbons and scraps of wrapping paper she and Cassie had missed during a quick cleanup. Nate's hand found her thigh, giving it a squeeze.

She'd never been happier.

After a minute, Sara's eyelids started to droop.

"What's that?" Nate's voice jolted her awake.

Pushing off his shoulder, she straightened. "What's what?"

"That." He pointed toward the fireplace. "Over there."

Squinting, Sara tried and failed to find anything out of place. "Where?"

"Your stocking." Arm still raised, his eyes cut to hers. "I think Santa came back."

Sara noted the lift at the corner of his lips. "He did, did he?"

Nate leaned back on the couch. "You better go see what he brought you."

Playing along, Sara pushed off the couch to stand and maneuvered around the coffee table toward the mantle. And when she lifted her red-and-green plaid stocking that she and Nate had picked out in a Christmas market in Victoria, it wasn't empty. "What did you do? You already gave me a gift this morning."

"That's not from me." Nate crossed one leg over the other. "Must be Santa."

"Uh-huh." Sara carried the stocking back to the couch with her, sliding out the gift once she sat down.

Sara's smile melted from shock when a small, black velvet box with a tiny bow on top toppled onto her lap.

"Oh." Nate plucked the box off her thighs, holding it up to the Christmas-tree light. "That *is* from me."

Sara opened her mouth, but nothing came out. She suddenly found it hard to breathe.

Dropping to his knee between the couch and coffee table, Nate opened the box. The single solitaire diamond glinted in the holiday lights.

"Not many people get more than one chance at true love

with the person they're meant to be with. Somehow you and I got three, and we've managed to not let this third one slip away." He removed the ring and set the box down beside him. "I love you, Sara Bennett." He lifted her left hand. "Will you turn this chance into a lifetime by becoming my wife?"

"Ye—" Sara cleared her throat, tight with emotion. Despite claiming earlier that she didn't need a ring, she hadn't realized how much she wanted one. This one. Along with Nate's perfect proposal. "Yes, of course I will."

He slipped the ring on her finger, but before he could say another word, Sara stood and pulled him to his feet.

"I love you." She went up on her toes and kissed him, then whispered, "I think I may have left one more gift for *you* upstairs. Want to go open it?"

* * * * *